Can Zack's shattered dreams for tomorrow
be made whole again?

As they walked through the upstairs bedrooms, Ruthella pictured each one in her mind with four-poster beds covered with quilted comforters and long floral draperies at the windows. When they came back downstairs her mind placed the hall benches and the coat hanging racks. The parlour was big enough to take a large-size sofa and she imagined lace curtains and brocade draperies at the tall windows. The kitchen wasn't too big—just big enough—with a huge fireplace on one wall. She would put. . . What was she doing? She blushed and realized she was furnishing the house in her mind!

"The kitchen will have a well right outside the back door. Many of the new homes in the east are starting to have water brought right into the home by pipes. I'm looking into that."

"Why, that would be wonderful!" Ruthella answered and felt her cheeks flush warm again.

They circled back to the entryway and walked out on the porch.

Zack stopped, turned to Ruthella, and grinned. "Well, what do you think of it?"

"Oh, Zack, it is elegant! Any woman would be thrilled having—a—home like—this." She felt her face grow warm with a blush.

NORENE MORRIS was born, as she says, "with a pencil in my hand." Morris makes her home in north-eastern Ohio and spends much of her time enjoying her grandchildren, as well as her great-grandchildren.

Books by Norene Morris

HEARTSONG PRESENTS
HP12—Cottonwood Dreams
HP39—Rainbow Harvest
HP107—Pioneer Legacy

Don't miss out on any of our super romances. Write to us at the following address for information on our newest releases and club information.

Heartsong Presents Readers' Service
P.O. Box 719
Uhrichsville, OH 44683

A Heart
for Home

Norene Morris

Heartsong Presents

To our Father, God,
Who placed us in families
to teach us to love.

A note from the Author:
I love to hear from my readers! You may write to me at the
following address:

Norene Morris
Author Relations
P.O. Box 719
Uhrichsville, OH 44683

ISBN 1-57748-050-3

A HEART FOR HOME

Cover illustration by Kathy Arbuckle.

PRINTED IN THE U.S.A.

one

"Tommy! Come back here!" Breathless, Mary Lou stopped when she saw Tom emerge from one of the corrals. To keep an eye on her son, Tommy, was a full-time job and to keep him occupied for any length of time with anything was nearly impossible. His sturdy legs beat double time to his mother's. He was almost to the point where he could outdistance her.

"Tommy! Obey your mother!" Tom's stern voice called from the barn door.

Tommy stopped in his tracks, darted a glance from one parent to the other, drooped his head, turned, and walked slowly back to his mother.

Mary Lou smiled and stretched out her hand when he reached her. "You're a good boy. Come help me gather the potatoes in the gunnysacks. Then you can go out to the barn and work with your father."

Tommy grabbed her hand and hopped along at his mother's side, a wide grin plastered across his eager little face. Tom and Mary Lou recognized the necessity of keeping four-year-old Tommy busy at useful tasks to teach him that life wasn't one big field to play in, with him in charge. His quick mind changed course by the moment, and his feet followed blindly where his mind directed.

"One of these days, he'll mesh the two together," Tom had assured Mary Lou on one particularly exasperating day.

Mary Lou sighed. *Yes, he will.* She recalled her adjustment to a whole new way of living as Tom's wife in her husband's big family. Her family had only been she, Pa, and Mama. Mostly Mama. Pa had spent most of his time riding Morgan out on the range, or he was away on a cattle drive.

Mary Lou couldn't contain her smile as Tommy bobbed up and down beside her singing "Jesus Loves Me." They moved surprisingly fast along the rows of potatoes turned above ground for harvest. When they plopped the last potato in its sack, Tommy turned and looked expectantly at his mother.

"We done, Mama?" Tommy stood poised to run.

Mary Lou surveyed the neat piles of sacks filled with potatoes piled at the end of each row and smiled at the eagerness of her son. She leaned and kissed his cheek. "Yes, we are!"

Tommy turned and shot off like a bullet. "I'm coming, Papa!" he shouted and seemingly flew to the barn.

Mary Lou watched her energetic son with pride. He had the exuberant energy and exactness of Tom, but to keep that energy focused was a major task. Any little bug or movement that captured his imagination was enough to coax him off course.

Tom appeared at the barn door and stood grinning as Tommy raced toward him. He waved overhead to Mary Lou, clamped his hand over his son's shoulder, and guided him into the barn.

Mary Lou waved back, heaved a sigh, and turned to her garden. Her small daughter, twin to Tommy, sat patiently between the bean rows, picking all the flowers from the middle of the rows and carefully placing them in her basket. The fact that they were generally known as weeds didn't daunt her enthusiasm. Beth picked another, squashed its blossom against her nose, smiled, then carefully added it to her basket of treasures.

Amused by her dainty daughter's actions, Mary Lou shook her head in amazement. No, it wasn't her imagination. Every day Beth *did* grow to look more like Mama. Thick, soft, chestnut curls bounced round her shoulders. One of Mary Lou's fond memories as a young girl was taking all the hairpins out of Mama's luxurious, brown wavy hair and watching it tumble down Mama's back. Then Mary Lou would brush and brush—

"Come, Beth," she called. She walked back to the house and washed her hands as she passed the pump. In the kitchen, she picked up the basket filled with half the cookies she had baked that morning with the dubious help of the twins. The shapes were interesting, the sizes not uniform, and they had a strong cinnamon taste, but she was sure they would disappear regardless.

Beth gathered herself and her flower basket then ran as fast as her little legs could travel over the irregular ground. She fell once, spilling her basket, lay in a surprised heap for a second, then undaunted, picked herself up, brushed her knees, and retrieved her scattered weed-flowers. She placed each one carefully into her basket and continued, mindless of the trail of weeds that escaped as she balanced her load and walked.

Mary Lou waited for her at the pump, washed Beth's hands and face, and dried her with her apron. Together they headed down the road to the main ranch, Beth chattering and skipping beside her mother like a frisky little puppy out for a morning romp. As they entered the gate, they saw Hattie moving up and down over her scrub board at the side of the house.

Hattie looked up suddenly. "'Bout time you came for

a visit. We was wonderin' if you still lived up there!"

Mary Lou nodded and laughed. "Yes, but there is just as much work to do up there as there is down here, only you have three women to do it!"

Hattie nodded sharply. "Just proves the old adage 'A man may work from sun to sun but a woman's work is never done,' " She said in singsong. "Might as well get used to it. But I wouldn't trade places with any one of them men with having to work from sunup to sundown to take care of their families—all them animals and crops plus doin' the buildin' and all the other work they do around here plus helpin' their neighbors." Hattie wrung the rinse water out of another pair of overalls and slapped them over the line to punctuate her observations.

Mary Lou caught a sparkle of tears. Hattie's husband must have been a good man. Sometimes when Hattie played with Tommy, Mary Lou wondered if she was thinking of her own little four-year-old son who had been killed by a bear. She walked over and put her hand on Hattie's shoulder. "Has anyone told you lately that we all thank God that He chose us for your second family?"

Hattie looked up, eyes sparkling over a warm smile and slowly nodded. "Don't have to. You all show it and I have thanked the good Lord every day of my life since I came here."

Mary Lou leaned over and kissed Hattie's wet cheek.

Beth raised her face for a kiss, too.

Hattie gathered the child in her arms, kissed her on both cheeks and forehead, squeezed her in a snuggle, set her back on her feet, then turned to her washtub.

As Mary Lou and Beth entered the ranch kitchen, Allena walked in from the hall. "Gamma!" Beth squealed and made a running dash to her grandmother.

"Here's my Bethie!" Allena cried and scooped her up into her arms, basket and all. "I was hoping you would come visit me today."

Beth responded with a squeal and stretched forth her basket of remaining treasures.

Allena feigned surprise. "For me?"

Beth giggled and nodded vigorously.

"They are beautiful. Thank you, Beth." Allena leaned over and set the basket with its tousled weeds in the middle of the kitchen table. "There!" she said. "Aren't they lovely?"

Mary Lou smiled. "Only a grandmother would do something like that. No wonder children like to visit Grandma."

Allena smiled and whispered, "Don't tell anyone, but grandmothers are notorious manipulators when it comes to their grandchildren's attention."

Lily walked into the kitchen, followed by Genevieve, who tottered in, toppled to the floor, then determinedly pushed herself back onto her feet and stood, weaving precariously, a triumphant grin spread across her delighted little face.

"She's walking!" Mary Lou cried.

Lily laughed. "If you can call it that. At this point it is an up-and-down business." Lily turned to Beth and stretched her arms wide. "And here's our sweet, little Beth! Come give Aunt Lily a big hug."

Beth obliged then pushed her away and turned to Genevieve. "Geevie," she cried and gave Genevieve a hug that toppled them both. They sat stunned for a moment then everyone laughed. Suddenly they realized they had done something to capture everyone's attention. They beamed, pushed themselves up on their feet and gleefully plopped to the floor again amidst the laughter.

Allena clapped her hands. "There is nothing as delightful as children. When my four boys were growing up, I could hardly wait until they were grown young men. But my grandchildren are growing up too fast! Sometimes nothing seems to be the way it ought to be." Allena nodded her head and smiled. "I think the good Lord in heaven often laughs not only at the children but us grownups as well. To Him we must act like silly children much of the time."

Everyone nodded agreement.

Mary Lou turned to Lily. "I really came to find out about your wedding. How is everything by now?"

"Well, Mother and I just finished my dress. I think I'm about as ready and I can be. Now it's up to the men to take time out for us to get married!"

"Have you set the day?" Mary Lou asked.

Lily nodded. "In between finishing our house and the fall roundup." She smiled and blushed. "That way we can get away from the three kids for a week."

The women burst into laughter.

Mary Lou threw her arms around Lily. "Sounds a little like the cart before the horse, but I agree! Tex is going to make a wonderful father for your darling little girl and those two sweet boys you have taken into your heart and home. Anyway, one thing we do thank Doug for, may his soul rest in peace, is the blessing of bringing you into this family."

Lily's eyes softened and became moist. " 'Tis I who am blessed." She batted tears from her eyes, bowed her head, and said no more.

Allena slid her arm around her shoulders. "And God blessed me with a daughter, a granddaughter, and two more dear, little boys in my old age. It takes most of us a good many years to discover that God has a way of making wrong things right, even though sometimes it takes us a long time to recognize His help."

The women were suddenly quiet.

The children looked up in wonderment. It was a hallowed moment.

two

Tom Langdon nudged Tinder toward the steep, treacherous trail up the north side of Langdon Mountain, which stood almost in the center of the family ranchland. It was small compared to the mountains to the west, stony and dangerous underfoot, but it commanded the best overall view of the Circle Z Ranch. Tom gave Tinder his head and let him pick and climb at his own speed.

Finally, the wary, sure-footed animal scrambled onto the smooth top of the mountain that looked as if a slice had been cut off the top to make a surprisingly smooth, sloping tabletop almost as flat as the plain below.

Tom dismounted and stroked and patted his panting horse. "Good boy, Tinder." He dropped the reins to the ground and stood surveying the expanse above and below, drinking in the breathtaking magnificence of the sky and land he loved. It had been worth the climb. How many times he and his tall, stately father had stood on this very spot, dreaming up the vision. Tom almost heard his father's resonant voice. *Take care of the land, son, and it will take care of you.* Tom now viewed the truth of his father's statement. The land now cared for not only one but four families.

The Circle Z ranch and range spread as far as Tom could see. Standing in the midst of it, Tom's whole being surged with fresh awareness of the depth of his father's love and satisfaction in the land. During those times he and his father had scanned the land from the top of Langdon Mountain, Tom now recognized that his father had deliberately imbedded in him a deep sense of pride, contentment, and the joy of ownership.

A quiet humility swept over Tom as his father's words flooded his mind. "God plants every man somewhere then coaxes and enables him to rise above the ordinary. Make sure, my son, that as you rise you remember whose son you are."

The first time his father had spoken thus Tom thought his father meant his son—Tom. Now he understood his father had meant Tom as a son of God.

Tom raised his eyes toward heaven. "God help me," he said aloud. "I want to honor You through Your gift of this land to my family. I pray to always be as honest and honorable in all my ways as my earthly father—" Tom bowed his head. "And my heavenly Father," he added softly.

A peaceful serenity enfolded Tom. He felt held in the arms of the whole scene while sky, land, and air poured energy into his soul and accelerated his spirit with a new sense of unexpected joy and anticipation. His body surged with new vigor, and his heart soared upward in a silent pulsing of gratitude to God.

Tom gazed across the whole Langdon spread and surveyed it with new eyes. It stretched out on all four sides of him and beyond what he could see.

To the north, the main ranch rambled expansively. Heat waves shimmered in the glaring afternoon sun from the roofs of its several large barns, corrals, stables, and the squat, sprawling ranch house which at the moment housed his mother, older brother Zack and Baby Zack, Laura and Nelson, his dead brother Doug's wife Lily and baby daughter Genevieve, and the two orphan Zigwald boys, Lars and Wilmot. A full house!

Tom grinned. And Hattie. Couldn't forget Hattie! She

was family. As a little boy, Tom had often been confused as to who his real mother was. He now knew he had become the substitute for Hattie's little boy who had been killed by a bear shortly after she lost her husband in the Civil War. All Tom knew was that he loved that loyal, big-hearted woman dearly. She, too, was family. But his crippled brother Nelson was the biggest surprise. What a change in his life after he married Laura! He was no longer a boy but a man in every sense of word and deed. What he couldn't handle physically, he engineered with his newly discovered imagination and mind. Laura was the perfect wife for him and treated him like a whole, healthy man and forced him to believe in himself. Most important, Laura made him *feel* like a man and had encouraged Nelson to tackle all he could in spite of his crutches.

"What makes a real man is in his heart!" Laura had announced one day in defense of Nelson. "If his heart is right with the Lord, he can't be anything else but the real man God intends him to be, no matter what the circumstances." She had tossed her head impatiently. "Humph! Nelson is more man than many I see struttin' around on two legs in Harness."

Tom laughed out loud and it echoed in the air. Laura was right. God bless her! She had fired Nelson with such confidence he had surprised even himself and had discovered within an acute business sense and innate knack for bookkeeping. Therefore, Zack put him in complete charge of the business side of the ranch, and his mother's long, fearful concern for her youngest son gave way to pride and open confidence and fostered a deep love and respect for her feisty daughter-in-law, Laura. Yes, the main ranch was in good hands.

Tom slowly turned south toward his own ranch with

its growing barns and buildings. In six years, his spread almost equaled the main ranch in size. A satisfied smile settled on Tom's face as he savored the joy of ownership and success in breeding two prize stallions that rivaled the best in the East. His father would have been proud. It also gave him confidence he was moving in the right direction in his aim toward his father's reputation as a breeder of prize stallions.

Time and scene faded and a quiet humility settled over Tom. His father's voice seemed to echo in the wind. "If a man's life crop is small he evidently hasn't been a very good farmer." Only now Tom intuitively understood what his father had meant and knew he would be right proud if he saw his Circle Z now.

Tom turned to the west and felt a wave of sadness as he looked at Zack's beautiful house that stood halted and as empty as the shell of his marriage. When the first shock of impending divorce papers had arrived in the mail from Darcy's father, if it hadn't been for Baby Zack, his brother would have lost all incentive to live. Tom watched his older brother withdraw even from his own family. He and Zack had always shared their successes or hurts, but now no one or nothing seemed to penetrate Zack's deep pain of Darcy's rejection.

At first, his brother had taken Baby Zack on long walks or horseback rides. Then abruptly he had cooped himself up in his office at Harness for weeks. Finally, he went to Boston to talk to Darcy, but neither his wife nor her father gave him audience. When Zack returned home, his pain had hung like a heavy, dark cloud over the whole family. Tom had ached for him so. The whole family had prayed.

Finally, Tom's gaze turned to the land in the east that had belonged to his dead brother, Doug. It had been deeded over to his only daughter, Genevieve. From where Tom stood now it looked as if a swarm of busy ants scrambled over a partially finished house that had seemingly sprouted overnight on top of a small rise on the land. Tom grinned. It had taken a determined shove from six-year-old Lars plus constant coaxing from that persistent boy before Tex had finally gathered up enough courage to ask Lily to marry him. Now Lars proudly declared to everyone, "Tex is gonna be my pa!" Tom even noticed a new softened look about Lily.

Tom grinned. "Yep," he said aloud, "Mother is right. Love does have a way of overcoming the worst obstacles."

Now all the women were in a flurry of sewing, cleaning, baking, buzzing and busying themselves with whatever it is women seem to have to do to get ready for a wedding.

Even nose-to-the-grindstone Smitty had been generous in allowing several of the cowhands free time to help Tex build his new ranch house. It almost seemed to have mushroomed overnight! "Course," the cowboys had joked at Tex, "we're only helpin' to get rid o' ya out of the bunkhouse so's there'll be some grub left fer the rest of us ta eat fer a change."

Tex took their joshing in good fun. He knew none of the boys meant a word of it. If the truth were known, Tex guessed they were a bit jealous of his good fortune, but would never have let on.

So, in no time at all a shell of four walls and a roof stood perched on top of a good-sized root cellar. A well had been dug, and Tex assured Lily of a good supply of water.

"A roof over my head and a well with water are the only two things I really need to start with," Lily had commented to Tex. "The good Lord will provide the rest as we need it."

Movement at his own ranch caught Tom's eye, and he whistled for Tinder. Mary Lou must be back home. The obedient horse trotted to his master's side and stood. Tom rubbed his forelock, patted Tinder's neck, mounted, reined him toward the path at the edge of the top, then trustingly gave him his head to seek his own footholds and choose his way back down.

When they finally reached level ground, man and animal seemed to be of the same mind to get home. At Tom's prompting Tinder broke into a frisky gallop and hightailed it toward the barn and a drink of water. Tom saw the small form of his wife emerge from the cabin door, look in his direction, then turn and walk back into the cabin.

Mary Lou opened the oven door, grabbed a couple of hot pads to remove the baked bread from the oven, and tipped the loaves out of their pans onto the wooden racks Tom had made for her last Christmas. She rubbed the crusty, fragrant loaves with a light coating of bacon grease then covered them with a cloth to soften the crust. She pulled her hanky out of her apron pocket, mopped her brow, and gladly stepped outside to catch a breath of cooler air. She faced the mountain, shaded her squinty eyes with her hands, searched for the tiny speck of her husband, and spotted him halfway down the mountainside.

She ran her hands over her hair to smooth its straying locks and sat down on her "restin' chair" as Tom called the old kitchen chair just outside her kitchen door. All was ready. Chicken stew simmered on her stove, awaiting dumplings. Mary Lou sighed. She'd just set a spell and seize the reward of a few precious moments at home by herself. There would be plenty of time after Tom got home to go down and get the twins from the main ranch. They always protested coming home at any time and much preferred being left at the main ranch to play with their cousins. Mary Lou grinned. They were now probably eating supper at their grandmother's table. She sighed and settled. It had been a long day—a long week of solid work. She and Tom could do with a quiet supper at home. Tom's face had looked strained and tired at breakfast this morning. Even the night's sleep had not erased the strain lines from his face. On top of the daily work of the ranch and helping to finish Tex and Lily's home, Tom was also deep in plans to add another bedroom and a dining room on the back of their cabin.

Mary Lou knew it would be such a help to be able to keep a table dressed and ready for company, as Allena did at the main ranch. Besides, she needed her kitchen table to work on. Tom and the cowboys promised Tex they would finish Tex and Lily's house so they and the children could get settled in after the wedding. Then the men would come and work on their house.

Mary Lou's gaze followed the moving speck of Tom and Tinder as they made their cautious descent toward the bottom of the mountain. She knew exactly when Tinder found his footing on level ground. From a snail's pace, he moved with a burst of speed and turned toward home.

She raised her eyes to the late afternoon sun. The quiet moment suddenly swelled her heart with love toward her heavenly Father for His gifts of a good, loving husband, two healthy children, a home, and a large loving family. Never in her wildest dreams could she have imagined her life to become what it had. Tears welled and spilled. Her heart and spirit soared her thanks to God for His love and kindness to her. Then it was almost as if The Lord received her praise then returned it to rest on her with a blessing of peace. "My cup runneth over," she said aloud and looked up. "Thank You, Father."

When Tom was near enough and she knew he could see her, she stood out a ways from the cabin and waved her arms over her head. Tom removed his Stetson and circled it high in answer; then Tinder broke into a full gallop.

By rights, instead of resting, she should have gone to get the twins. But there were so few times when she and Tom were alone during any day. She selfishly decided to snatch another hour so she and Tom could have a quiet supper together. Then they would both go to the main ranch for the twins.

three

As Tom approached the barn he heard a roar of laughter from the cowboys inside. Suddenly Tex hoofed it out the door, his face the color of a ripe tomato. He looked mighty mad.

"What's up, Tex?"

"Nothin'."

"If it's the cowboys joshin' you, don't pay attention to them. They're jealous that it isn't one of them that's getting married next week." Tom fell in step with Tex as he hustled toward the corral. "Wanna take a ride and cool off?"

A quick, sharp nod spoke Tex's consent.

They saddled their mounts in silence, and the routine job of saddling his horse seemed to calm Tex. His jaw relaxed and he glanced sideways at Tom now and again. A half grin finally crossed his face.

They rode off at a smooth, easy trot until the barns were out of sight then slowed to a walk.

"I never was good at joshin'," Tex commented. "When I was growin' up, my pa didn't allow no foolishness—"

Tom laughed. "Aw, Tex, don't let them get to you. In one week they will be green-eyed, watching you head home to your own place with a nice home-cooked meal and a pretty woman awaitin'—and don't let them tell you any different. Come on, Tex, they're just trying to get a rise out of you."

Tex grinned. "Well, they did."

The men turned their horses in the direction of the

new house being erected on the land straight ahead.

"The roof will be finished tomorrow, and Lily wants to start moving some stuff in already. But—there's so much more to do." The tone of Tex's voice bespoke bewildered confusion.

Tom laughed. "Tex, you gotta learn that a woman has to settle. We men are used to sleeping on the ground with a saddle for a pillow with a blanket wrapped around us to keep warm. My father told me women like it to be soft and smell clean and soaplike. Mother calls it 'nesting'."

Embarrassed, Tex ducked his head, nodded, and grinned.

They rode together in silence, watching Tex and Lily's new home loom closer and closer.

Tom thought back to when he and Mary Lou were married. It certainly hadn't been the usual wedding! Before it all ended happily ever after he remembered wondering whether he or Glenn would end up as her husband. Tom grinned. He understood all too well the anxiety Tex was going through. Even in a normal wedding a man taking on a wife was a big step!

"You have a mother and father someplace, Tex? I've never heard you mention them. I'm sure they would like to know you are marrying a good woman."

The clip-clop of the horses' hooves filled the silence for a short piece, then, voice husky, Tex said, "My pa was killed in the Civil War and my ma in an Indian attack when we was comin' west with the wagon train. I was only seven then so the family we was ridin' with just took me in. They was good folks. They treated me kindly just like their own."

Tom's eyes widened and he suppressed a grin. That was the longest speech Tom had ever heard Tex make since he'd hired him. "Soon as I was eleven I hooked up with some cowpunchers, and they learned me the tricks. Been on my own ever since."

"So that's why you're such a good cowhand! I know I'm right proud to have you a part of the Circle Z."

Tex shot an appreciative glance at Tom, ducked his head, and grinned in embarrassment. "Yeah. I like it, too."

They plodded along in silence. Tom turned toward Tex. "I don't know about you, but my stomach's telling me the women will probably have dinner about ready." Tom said. "Let's find out."

They swung their horses, called a "tch," and headed them toward the new ranch house. The animals' hooves pounded the ground in rythmic cadence as the new house grew larger and larger.

Lily stepped out the open doorway, shaded her eyes with her hands, then suddenly waved both arms over her head.

The men pressed their mounts into a moderate gallop till they reached the new sturdy hitching rail, dismounted, and flopped their reins around it.

Lars came running out the door to Tex. "Where you been? Lily wouldn't let me go find you."

"I was working at the ranch, Lars. Did you help Lily with chores around here, like I told ya?"

"Yes, he did." Lily answered. "He carried water and chopped some wood and—"

Tex smiled and tousled the boy's hair. "You're going to be some good, big, strong cowpuncher come one of these days."

Lars stretched taller and straightened his shoulders. His face beamed and he followed Tex around the house.

Lily greeted Tom. "Mary Lou came today and thanks to her we have the wedding all planned." She smiled and lowered her eyelids.

Tom looked at the pretty woman standing in front of him and his mind harkened back to the day his brother, Doug, had brought Lily home as his wife. She had been dressed in the revealing clothes all the saloon girls wore but in all decency had hugged a fringe shawl around her bare shoulders and arms. It had been a shock to the whole family, but true to form, his mother had opened her heart and her arms, accepted Lily as Doug's wife, and finally brought her to the Lord. He gazed now at the beautiful woman before him who vaguely resembled that girl Doug had brought home. Many people who knew her then would be hard put to recognize her today. Tom marveled at what God and the love of a family had done for this one soul. His gaze caught hers.

Lily smiled then lowered her eyes.

Was she remembering, too? Was he embarrassing her? "Well, Lily," he asked expectantly, "when did you decide the wedding day will be?"

"Mother said we could probably figure a week or so and that Tex had better see to the legal fixings." Lily blushed.

Did Tom imagine it or had he heard Tex gulp?

"My dress is all ready, and Hattie has even begun some of the cooking." Suddenly, Lily shot an anxious look toward Tex. "Did you tend to all the legal papers today?"

Tex turned and shot a desperate look of "help!" to Tom.

Tom laughed and patted Tex on the back. "Don't worry, Lily. You women take care of the wedding and home fussin', and we men will have all the right papers to make it legal."

Lily flushed and gazed at her feet. "I'm sorry." Harking back to Lily's marriage to Doug, it was only natural Lily would have some anxiety. Even though dead, Tom's brother Doug stamped even this marriage with his usual unpleasant mark.

Movement turned Tom's head. A wagon was leaving the main ranch. Even though it was too far away to see clearly, he figured Jeff, the bunkhouse cook, was at the reins of the chuck wagon, probably driving up with dinner for everyone. He turned to Tex. "Seems we got here right on time. Here comes dinner."

The gentle *clop, clop* of a horse's hooves caught Tom's attention. Mary Lou had seen Tom and Tex riding toward the new ranch house. She figured the family would be gathered there and would be eating together. Tom hurried to lift her from the horse.

All work ceased. Everyone washed up and hunted for a seat. There were only two chairs made so the men settled long boards across wooden horses and nail kegs. By the time the chuck wagon arrived all were ready and stood waiting. Everyone dished up from the wagon, and the makeshift benches were soon filled.

Tom helped his mother and the children get settled then sat Tex at the head of his first dinner table in his own home and sat down beside him.

Tex stared straight ahead, his face flushed, then turned desperate eyes to Tom.

Tom read their message, grinned, and glanced around at the expectant faces. "Well, now, I can't think of a better time to put a blessing on this house than right now. Let's bow our heads."

A hush fell as all heads bowed.

Tom raised his face to heaven. "Father God, we thank Thee for Thy blessings of home and family. We thank Thee for the blessing of this land You gave to my father for his family to use as their home on this earth. Now we ask Thy blessing upon this new home and the new family it will shelter. Thank You for this good food prepared for us. May it make us strong in Thy service. In Jesus' name, Amen."

Everyone looked up and Tom noticed a sparkle of tears in his mother's eyes as they rested upon him.

She blinked, smiled, and nodded her approval.

Tom grinned in return. A tender memory surfaced of his father's dignity and command even at a dinner table. Father had always said grace, but every so often he would call on one of the boys to do it. In turn they had each squirmed and sputtered but gradually learned to pray at the table. Only twelve at the time of his father's death, he had been too young to appreciate what an important role a man and father plays in a family.

Suddenly Tom sensed the tremendous loss his mother must have felt when his father died, so much so that she had never allowed anyone to sit in his chair or take his place at the dinner table, a visible reminder of his absence.

Zack had said grace until he left to go East to study law. Doug had always refused to say grace or wasn't home, so it had filtered down to Tom. Funny, Tom had never thought about it before. Now as he watched his mother shift into her role as gracious hostess even at a makeshift, wooden table in a half-built house, a rush of love and respect for her flooded him. As always she sat with an endearing, cheerful smile, a concern for her family's needs always uppermost in her mind. *O God,* Tom prayed, *give my mother a double blessing.*

"Tom! Don't you want any of these potatoes?"

Tom snapped back to the present and grabbed the pan of rolly, browned potatoes stretched toward him. He dumped several spoonfuls on his plate and passed them to Tex. Their eyes met in new understanding.

four

The twins took off on a run ahead of Mary Lou as they neared the main ranch house.

Suddenly the ranch kitchen door swung open, and Lily marched out wearing a face like a storm cloud. She stopped abruptly when she saw the twins, scooped up each one as they reached her, swung them in a high circle, then replaced them on the ground.

They squealed and made a giggling beeline for the ranch kitchen door. Like a little gentleman, after much training from his father, Tommy opened the door for Beth to go through, followed her in, and ran to Baby Zack.

Lily, her face like a mask, walked briskly toward Mary Lou. When they met, Lily linked her arm through Mary Lou's. "Want to go for a walk?" Lily's eyes pleaded, her lips trembled, and the irritation in her voice told Mary Lou she needed not only to walk off some steam but to talk it out as well.

Mary Lou pointed toward the clump of Texas umbrella trees. "Why don't you go out there and sit in the shade and cool off a bit? I'll be ready to set a spell as soon as I say hello to Mother and Hattie." She reached and squeezed Lily's hand for assurance as she left her.

Mary Lou entered the kitchen and immediately guessed Lily's problem. Allena was busy bathing and dressing Genevieve.

Hattie, with hanging floury hands, bent over Beth, who had evidently thrown her arms around Hattie's skirts to give her a hug. Tommy already had his arm around Baby Zack's shoulders. Both were eyeing two little wooden toy horses Wilmot was playing with that Tex had carved for him.

"Hello," Mary Lou called as she entered. "Just what you need, a couple more children."

"The more the better," Allena said. "Now I understand what my grandmother used to mean when my brother and I came to visit. She used to call us the 'joys of her life'." She made a wide sweep with her arm. "Now these are my joys."

Mary Lou stood beside Allena as she washed and splashed with Genevieve. "Looks like you're busy right now. I met Lily as I came in. I need to ask her a couple questions about the wedding and see how our bride-to-be is holding up."

"Not too well," Allena commented. She lifted Genevieve out of the bath pan and enfolded her in a large flannel blanket.

Mary Lou smiled. "Shucks, all brides are allowed the jitters. I know I had them. Heavens! It's the biggest step any woman ever takes." Mary Lou bent over and kissed the sweet baby Genevieve, who wiggled impatiently while her grandmother rubbed her dry.

Hattie glanced from one to the other like the wise old bird she was but never opened her mouth.

Mary Lou found Lily sitting on the ground with her back leaning against a tree trunk that sheltered her from the hot sun with its dense shade of motionless leaves. She sensed Lily's distress, dropped to her knees, lifted Lily's downturned face, and smiled. Lily pinned an intense, troubled look on Mary Lou but didn't speak.

Mary Lou sat down beside her. *She's very angry about something.* It was written on her face and confirmed by the rigid set of her body, arms crossed tight in containment.

"Was Grandmother bathing *her* baby granddaughter?" Lily spit out the words.

Mary Lou heard Lily's irritation, felt her hurt. "Yes."

"Sometimes I wonder whose baby Genevieve is. Hers or mine."

So it had finally come to the boiling point. Mary Lou had expected it long before this and had admired Lily's generosity and patience in sharing her little daughter with her grandmother. Ever since Lily and Genevieve had been found, Mary Lou had noticed a growing tension between her mother-in-law and sister-in-law.

She understood Allena's joy in caring for her precious granddaughter after having longed for a baby girl all the while she raised four boys.

Mary Lou also recalled Allena's delight in Laura before she and Nelson announced their intention to be married. It had been difficult for the family to understand Allena's vigorous opposition to Laura and Nelson's marriage. Though Nelson's body was not strong, his spirit had displayed vigorous strength. He had stood adamant and informed his mother that if Laura wasn't welcomed as his wife on the Circle Z then they would live elsewhere.

To be honest, even Mary Lou had seriously questioned the wisdom of their marriage, but both she and Tom had supported Nelson and Laura because they loved each other and their love would surmount the obstacles. It had taken some strong talk to finally convince Allena that marriage would be a good thing for both of them.

To Allena's credit, after their first year she had acknowledged that Laura had given Nelson what she could never have given him. His manhood.

Lily suddenly covered her face with her hands, bowed her head, and let the tears roll. Her shoulders rose and fell with whimpering sobs.

Mary Lou slid an arm around her and sat quietly patting her shoulder, waiting for her to cry it out. What was it about women? Sometimes the only thing that relieved any situation was a good cry. Mama used to say tears were a blessing from God that gathered up all our hurts and washed them away.

Lily's sobs gradually subsided. She glanced up into Mary Lou's face and smiled through her embarrassment. "Just like some little child who runs to Mama with her hurts," she sniffed.

Mary Lou grinned, gave her an extra sqeeze, pulled a handkerchief out of her apron pocket, and handed it to Lily. "I am a mama. In your case, I'm the handy substitute." She lifted Lily's face and looked into her teary eyes. "But after you and Tex are married, you'll find your most comforting place will be in your husband's arms. At least that is the way it has been for me." Mary Lou hadn't thought about that before but it was true. Early in their marriage Tom's arms became not only Mary Lou's place of love but of rest and peace also.

Suddenly an old memory crossed Mary Lou's mind. Even as a child, she had never remembered any time ever seeing her father hold her mother in his arms! *Oh, Mama. How did you stand it? Pa was gone so much of the time. . .but even when he was there. . .* The precious love she shared with Tom overwhelmed her heart. She gazed into Lily's teary eyes and tried to spill some of her overflow of love into the agony of Lily's sadness.

Lily daubed her tears with Mary Lou's handkerchief and smiled feebly. "In all my life, I don't remember anyone's arms being there for me except for all the wrong reasons, so maybe I don't really know what I'm looking for."

Mary Lou laughed. "Oh, Lily, you are just having bride jitters. Lord willin', you will have the love you seek when you marry Tex. He worships the ground you walk on." Mary Lou laid her hand across Lily's. "Lily, forget about your past. Your past doesn't mean anything to him. It is truly past. Forget it! Tex loves you as you are, and you're the woman who loves him. That's what it takes to make a marriage, Lily, two people deeply in love accepting and loving each other as they are, regardless of what they may have been. It won't work any other way."

Lily slowly nodded then glanced up, a new light of understanding shining in her misty eyes. She smiled and wiped away her tears. "I'm going to make Tex the best wife in the world."

Mary Lou nodded and gave Lily a reassuring pat. "I know you will. I'm happy for Tex, too, 'cause I remember the day a young cowboy named Tex helped me hang curtain rods when Tom and I were finishing up our house. I thanked him for his help and the good job he did. He smiled and wistfully spoke with yearning of wanting a wife and his own spread someday just like Tom's. Just from the way he said it, I felt he would make some sweet, loving woman a good husband and began praying she would come."

Mary Lou cupped Lily's face in her hands. "You are that woman, Lily."

"Me!" Lily covered her face and shook her head. But—"

"No buts. Just love him. That's what he wants and needs. Let him know you love him. Tell him every day." Mary Lou laughed. "Lily, if you can't see the love pouring from that cowboy's eyes when he looks at you, you are blind! It has to be love with a lot of courage in Tex's heart to take on the job of not only caring for the woman he loves but to immediately assume a ready-made family of a baby and two orphan boys! Lily, you are a blessed woman!"

Lily stared at Mary Lou through her tears and slowly nodded acceptance of a new discovery. "Yes, I am," she said softly. Her lips parted in amazement. "I am!" She raised her eyes toward heaven. "Thank You, Lord, for giving me a family. Now I'm counting on You to help me to become the woman You want me to be."

"—and Tex needs," Mary Lou added.

The two women fell into each other's arms, hugged, rose and walked back toward the house.

Suddenly, Lily stopped and nodded. "Perhaps now I understand how much Genevieve means to Mother. I am so thankful for Allena. I don't know where I would be today except for her. But Mary Lou, I just want to care for my baby. Is that so wrong?" she asked wistfully.

"Of course not. I understand how you feel, Lily. But you must also consider something else. Genevieve is Allena's only link to her dead son, regardless of how unruly a son he became. He gave her nothing but shame and heartache when he was alive. Remember Genevieve is all that is left of her son Doug. That dear, sweet baby girl is the only blessing Doug ever gave her. That could be one reason why she hovers over Genevieve." In a moment of silence between them, Mary Lou remembered harboring those same feelings toward Allena after her twins were born. She decided to tell Lily to help her understand.

"I remember how wonderful and gracious Mother was to me when Tom brought me home as his wife, sight unseen. To make things worse, I was the second strange new wife. Zack had arrived with Darcy six months or so before Tom brought me. Then Doug came home one morning married to you, a dance-hall girl. Lily, she's had some tough pills to swallow. But Allena is a strong lady with lots of love and graciously accepted us all under her roof and calls us her family."

Lily stared wide-eyed at Mary Lou. "I never knew. . ."

Mary Lou laughed. "Well, it isn't exactly dinner-table conversation! Not only that, Lily, Tom and I lived in the main ranch house when we had the twins. I admit there were times I felt she monopolized them. She was so capable. I had been an only child and hadn't grown my new-mother wings yet. I learned so much from Allena. At that particular time, her loving concern and help was a lifeline for me."

Mary Lou cupped Lily's chin in her hand and looked directly into her misty eyes. "And I harbored some of your same feelings until we moved out of the main ranch into our own house."

Lily's wide eyes softened.

Mary Lou laughed. "Just wait, Lily. After you're married, you will have Genevieve all the time. You probably won't believe this now, but there will be days when you will be eager for Allena to come and take her away so you can get some of your work done in peace and quiet. She will become a blessing in disguise." A calm sigh of release softened the expression in Lily's eyes, and Mary Lou knew she had gotten her message across.

"So," Mary Lou patted Lily's hand. "Can't you let your heart loan Genevieve to her grandmother for just a little while longer until you take her home with you and Tex after you are married?"

"I'm sorry." Lily bent her head. "I sound so ungrateful.

I'm not—really—but I was afraid Genevieve would not remember that *I* am her mama. When she wakes every morning I have to fight to be the first one up to get her so I can change and dress her. The only time I get her is nursing time."

Mary Lou suddenly pulled Lily into the comfort of her mother arms and cradled her as she would one of her twins. *Sometimes mothers have to mother other mamas.* The obvious truth of the thought startled her. Then she remembered Mama had said that.

"We aren't the only ones, Lily. My mama and aunt Tibby knew the agony of hurtful family feelings. They had been ripped away from their mama and disowned by their father's anger for what he called his daughters' disobedience. Their crime? They had chosen to marry the men they loved. Grandfather never accepted either of their marriages. Even their names were never allowed to be mentioned in his presence. I saw Grandmother only once when Mama, Aunt Libby, and I went to Grandma's funeral. Mama and Aunt Tibbie found all the letters they had written to their mother and father hidden in an old trunk, unopened.

"And, of course, I've told you that my pa did not approve or accept my marriage to Tom. It was only this past year when we traveled back to Kansas to visit my family that Pa accepted Tom as my husband and the father of his grandchildren. Pa had been a cowboy and had wanted someone better for me, he said. When he recognized what a good husband and father Tom is and fell in love with his grandchildren, all was forgiven."

The memory of Pa with Beth and Tommy perched on his knees brought tears to Mary Lou's eyes. How grateful she was for that sweet memory. "So you see, Lily, without Aunt Tibby and Aunt Nelda's blessings I wouldn't be where I am today, the wife of the man I love and the mother of our beautiful twins."

Lily's eyes stared wide with surprise. "I didn't know all that."

Mary Lou reached over with a fresh hanky out of her apron pocket and patted Lily's teary cheek.

"I'm sorry," Lily said softly and sniffed. "I sound so ungrateful."

Mary Lou shook her head. "Nothing to be sorry about. Mama always said that every so often a woman has to have a good cry and doesn't need any reason except that she needs a good cry."

Lily's moist eyes clung to Mary Lou's. "Believe me, I love Mother Allena. If she told me once she has said a dozen times, 'I always wanted a daughter—'"

"And there is nothing wrong with that, Lily. But perhaps you ought to pray to learn to trust your new family. . ."

Lily pulled a handkerchief out of her apron pocket and daubed her eyes, lifted her chin and grinned. "I *am* Genevieve's mother and nothing can change that." She slowly shook her head back and forth. "I'm ashamed for being so ungrateful. If Mother has told me once, she has said it a dozen times. 'I always wanted a daughter.' Lily swallowed hard. "And she had meant me!"

Lily lifted her face toward the sky. "God, please forgive me for my selfishness. Nothing can change the fact that I am Genevieve's mother, but without this family, I would never have had her. Dear Jesus, teach me to give of me and mine as You gave Yourself for me."

"Amen," Mary Lou said softly. Both women rested in the quiet blessing that hung graciously in the air.

Abruptly, Lily stood up, reached and pulled Mary Lou to her feet. "Enough of this. I've had my little pity party." She put her arm around Mary Lou. "Thank you for giving me your shoulder to cry on."

Mary Lou grinned and hugged her. "That's what sisters are for."

Lily nodded. Her eyes held a fresh knowing.

The two girls walked slowly back to the ranch house. When they entered the kitchen, Genevieve squealed and toddled toward her mother, arms outstretched, "Ma-ma!"

Lily picked her up and swung her around. "Here's my sweet girl. My, aren't you pretty! Your grandma made you look so beautiful."

Allena turned from dishing up oatmeal and smiled. "Come, breakfast is late so let's all sit down. Jess fixed breakfast real early for the men so they could get up to your house, and we will all take dinner up in the chuck wagon to eat up there. Hattie and I promised to bring chicken and biscuits and pies."

Mary Lou watched her mother-in-law and Hattie move from stove to table with bowls of oatmeal. Women and children took their places, grace was said, and the new day began.

Before the week was out Jess drove the ladies to Harness for final supplies for the wedding.

Lily's simple but beautiful wedding dress, covered with a sheet, hung on a hook on her bedroom wall. All was ready. Lily and Tex would be married on the coming Saturday.

five

Tom opened the gate to the corral, led Adam through, and tied him on a long rope to continue his training and gain control of the abundant energy of Tommy's frisky colt. As the animal took advantage of the full length of the training rope, Adam noticed his sleek, well-proportioned form. Good thing that he had given in to Tommy's daily pestering to "ride my horse."

The young colt pranced briskly around the corral, straining and slacking the rope, his muscles rippling as he tossed his head in rhythm with his strong stride. Tom reined him in, smoothed the saddle pad over his back and saddled him. The first time Adam felt the saddle he had turned his head in sudden surprise, skittered a bit but soon settled with Tom's encouragement. Now Adam seemed ready to take everything in stride so Tom felt he was ready for his new master. Today was the day that young master would begin *his* training and be made ready for his horse.

Tom harkened back to when he was young and grinned. Up until he was four, his father often rode Victor with him on the saddle in front of him. Tom had done the same with Tommy on Tinder to pass his good memory on to his son.

Tom was five when his father gave him his first horse. Her name was Buttercup. She had served the Circle Z well over the years but in reality was a slow, docile, old nag. Yet to Tom she became the most magnificent horse in the world because she was his and they traveled the whole ranch. Sometimes his father let him ride with him when he and the cowboys looked for calves in the spring. He remembered how grown up and tall in the saddle he had felt but was disappointed when he couldn't chase cows. That activity was beyond Buttercup anyway.

One day, when Tom and Buttercup were out riding with the boys she missed her footing on a slippery hill, stumbled, fell and broke her leg. The memory of that day had remained a gripping, sorrowful remembrance of a horrible ache in his chest as her pain-filled eyes had reached out and pleaded for help. When Smitty got ready to shoot Buttercup, his father sent Tom back to the barn, riding double with one of the cowboys.

The impact of the shot that severed him from his friend had felt like a bullet in own heart. He had cringed with the pain of it and had bit his lip to keep from crying. When the cowboy dropped him off at the barn and headed back to the boys, Tom, blinded by tears, had walked like a big man until he was out of sight then had run, dropped into a crumbled heap behind the bunkhouse, and cried his hurt out until there were no more tears. After that he rode other horses but they were never the same. Until Tinder.

On Tom's twelfth birthday his father had walked him to the barn and introduced him to a sleek, shiny, black gelding. On his back sat a handsome new leather saddle similar to his father's but not quite as big. Tom's mind had exploded with joy. His own horse! His own saddle! Those first joyous moments of sitting in his own saddle on his own horse bonded boy and horse together, and they soon learned to move as one.

But Tom's father had made it absolutely clear that Tinder was Tom's sole responsibility to feed, water, brush, ride, exercise, and keep his horse's stall clean. He remembered how grown up he had felt yet the responsibility of the daily chores wore a bit thin after a few months. He had never realized what constant attention and work a horse required of its master.

Looking back, it had all been worth it. Tom had been able to join his father and the cowboys in the next roundup and began to shoulder a man's work. He smiled. His life had now come full circle, and he wanted those same vibrant memories for his son.

Using his father's wisdom, Tommy, at five, had been given Amber, an old plow horse who had served the family well. Tom recognized that his son's unbounded, imaginative energy needed early curbing. So far, old Amber was doing a good job of tempering his impatient son. Every so often, mindless of the consternation of her master, Amber stood in place until her rheumatism released her to move forward. No matter how hard Tommy plagued her, the old nag just ignored him and let the boy stew in his frustration. The young cowboy also learned she was always her most cooperative when she headed toward home to her stall to be fed and cared for by her young master. Tommy handled her surprisingly well.

The cowboys got a big charge out of the two of them as they fought the daily battle as to who was boss.

Tom smiled remembering one day Tommy had stomped into the barn, his lips pursed under his fuming nose.

"Where's your horse?" Tom asked immediately.

Tommy pointed, "Out there!" and stood defiant in front of his father. "Not gonna ride Amber no more. She won't listen."

Tom surpressed a smile and looked sternly at his son.

"You mean you left your horse?"

Tommy's pouting mouth receded at the accusing tone of his father's reprimand. His eyes grew cautious before his father's scowling face.

"A real cowboy *never* leaves his horse!" Tom had thundered. "Now you get back out there, find Amber, and bring her into the barn, take off her saddle, brush her, and put her out to pasture. Until you can treat that horse the way she ought to be treated, you ride no more."

Tommy had stared wide-eyed at his father's thundering face. He had never seen him so angry, had never heard such fury in his voice. It riveted him to the spot.

"Now *git!*" Tom had commanded.

A loud squeal from the ranch house broke into Tom's reverie. He turned to see his son running pell-mell toward the barn, followed by Beth trying to keep up with him and Mary Lou walking behind. Tom grinned. He guessed it was as good a time as any to start Adam and Tommy's training. He was a bit young, but Tom felt he needed a strong challenge.

At the fence, Tommy scrambled to the top. Mary Lou lifted her daughter and helped her plant her feet firmly over a cross board so she could hang on to see over the top rail.

"Adam looks great," Mary Lou called to Tom then lifted her nose in the air with posed pride. "And I see Eve has been doing pretty well herself. She never flinched when you added that saddle the other day." Mary Lou laughed. "She's a dainty copy of Adam."

"She'll be a sweet, gentle filly for Beth." Tom waved to his daughter, and she waved back wildly.

"Pretty soon, Papa and I will help you learn to ride Eve, and she will be your horse," Mary Lou told her softly.

"Eve is my horse," Beth called to Tommy.

Tommy was too engrossed in Adam to even hear her.

Mary Lou smiled in pride. *Tommy sits Adam well. Shades of his father,* she thought. Her heart skipped a beat. His stirrups were up as high as they could go. A tinge of sadness yet relief washed over Mary Lou when she realized her son would soon be his father's constant companion. She had completed her first and main task. She had birthed and fed him and taught him about Jesus during these first five years. Soon she would have to wean herself from her son and pass him to his father. Yet her heart didn't feel sad. It felt proud! She'd be helping him with his schoolwork, but Tom would be his main teacher to guide him in the ways of men, and by the time he was twelve he would be gone for weeks at a time riding the range of the Circle Z with the men. Her father had said, "time waits for no man." *Nor woman,* Mary Lou thought as she looked at Beth.

Her mother's heart reached for her Father in heaven. *But this is the way you planned it, Lord, and called it good. Bless our children, heavenly Father, to the task you have in mind for them in this life. Help Tom and me to teach them to love You so they will grow to be the man and woman You created them to be.*

She glanced at Beth, hanging on the fence, her face as usual a picture of delight at anything her twin brother did.

Tom walked Adam around and around, paused, slapped his rump, talked to him, rubbed the colt's neck and forelock, and smoothed his velvety nose. Tommy mimicked his father's every move.

Suddenly Tom stooped, picked up his son and slid him into the saddle. "Adam, you and this boy of mine are going to have a great time together, so I want you to know each other real good."

Adam swung his head around to see the featherweight on his back. Tom circled again talking and encouraging Tommy to lean forward and pat Adam's neck and talk to him. "He needs to get used to the sound of your voice, son. Before long he'll know it from anywhere."

"Let's go," Tom called and sent Adam off with a light pat on his rump then eased the rope as Adam trotted around at the end of it.

Tommy's eyes widened. A big smile spread across his face as Adam walked steadily around and around.

Tom turned and grinned at Mary Lou. "Any good horse senses when he has a greenhorn on his back, be it man or boy."

Both parents laughed.

Beth laughed too. Her wide eyes watched her brother's every move. She turned to her mother. "Me, too, me, too!"

Mary Lou cupped her little chin. "Pretty soon, Beth, pretty soon we'll teach you to ride Eve, your horse."

Beth turned her radiant face to Tommy and shouted. "I'm gonna ride Eve!" she called.

Tommy straightened in the saddle, gave her a broad grin, and proclaimed, "I'm riding Adam!"

Mary Lou's heart warmed. They were proud of each other! There was an unmistakable bond. Was it because they were twins and had shared the same womb? Whatever created the bond, it always made her proud whenever she watched Tommy protect his twin sister as they played.

Cradled in the comfort and presence of her little family, Mary Lou's heart burst into prayer. *O Lord, let me share the joy you've given me with others!* She bowed her head in silent benediction.

six

The ranch kitchen door swung wide as Lily and Genevieve greeted the bright morning sun, squinting, and walked toward it hand in hand.

"We gonna pick fwowers, Mama?" Genevieve asked as she skipped beside her mother. Her curly, brown hair bounced on her shoulders.

"Yes, we are. Let's see if we can pick a nice bouquet for me to carry when I marry Tex tomorrow and one for you to carry in your basket and some extra flowers to decorate the house." Lily grinned. *Rare is the bride who goes into the field to pick her own wedding bouquet with her daughter skipping at her side.*

Genevieve suddenly released her mother's hand and ran pell-mell toward a cluster of Texas bluebonnets swaying in the soft morning wind.

"Fwowers, Mama!" The child stood poised for her mother's response.

"Yes, they're beautiful. Pick some of those." Lily hugged her shawl around her body to keep out the gusty early morning air that still carried some of its night chill.

It didn't seem to daunt Genevieve's enthusiasm. The delighted child flitted from flower to flower like a selective butterfly, picking some with long stems and roots, others only inches from their blossom.

Lily smiled and squelched a reprimand. How dare she spoil the exuberance of her daughter just because her emotions were on edge? The thought of this being her last day to call the main ranch house "home" sent scary shivers up and down her back and resurrected memories of being passed from pillar to post most of her childhood, depending on who claimed her. The Circle Z was the only place she had ever felt any sense of security.

From that first frightening day when Doug brought her home from the saloon as his wife, her life had taken a new shape. Lily had thanked God for a mother-in-law who with gracious poise had taken all in stride and had accepted Lily as her son's wife regardless of who and what she had been. She knew it hadn't been easy. At first Lily remembered how confused and unhappy she had been, never knowing what to expect from Doug. He had dumped her on his family shortly after they were married, went back to the life he'd always led in town at the saloon, and finally spent little or no time with her or the ranch.

Gradually, surrounded by the love of his family, who had accepted her as Doug's wife, Lily gratefully had relaxed. Allena encouraged her to become her real self. In reality, who was she? Lily hadn't really known.

But it had been the first time in her life Lily had felt what it was like to be safe and loved. Allena had treated her with the same respect she gave her other daughters-in-law. Lily remembered living with her heart in her mouth her first month at the ranch, waiting to be thrown out. Even now, on the day before her wedding, she remained completely overwhelmed by the love of the Langdon family and their loyalty to each other.

Strange, she hadn't thought of Doug for a long time. Today, for some reason her mind kept returning to that horrible morning Doug had brought her home after their hasty marriage by a judge. She would never have gone through with it if she hadn't been so desperate, willing to do anything to escape her life at the brothel. When she finally stood in front of his mother, Hattie, and Mary Lou, their skirts to the ground, she remembered clutching her black fringed shawl around her bare shoulders and arms and wishing her dress had been at least below her knees. Even now she inwardly cringed remembering how uncomfortable and out of place she had felt. But Doug didn't change. She saw very little of him since he spent the same amount of his time at the saloon. At first, Lily couldn't figure out why he seemed to want to hurt his mother so much. It took only a few months of married life to discover that Doug hurt everything he touched and that he had no more consideration of her as his wife than he had for his mother or any other person, man or woman. He had moved in and out of her life as it pleased him, never had considered her feelings, told her where he was going, where he had been, what he was doing nor when he would return, nor did he leave any money for her needs. His only gifts to her had been to bring her to his home and give her Genevieve.

Lily shook her head. What on earth had prompted her mind to dig up all those unpleasant memories on the day before her wedding? She thought she had deeply buried her old life, but periodically it rose to haunt her.

Allena had helped her with that, too. After a particularly humiliating time with Doug, Mother had told her to bury all her hurts and anger in a grave of forgiveness, then helped her do it. It had been the first time in her life that Lily had known what it was to feel a mother's loving care and concern.

Yet Lily had tossed and turned last night, apprehensive on her next-to-last night under the safe, loving Langdon roof. The old feeling of impermanence and insecurity that had dogged her all her life snuck up and scratched for entrance to shake her present security. Did she really know Tex well enough to trust herself and her daughter into his care? Were most brides as frightened as she was? Her eyes followed her daughter darting here and there as Genevieve carefully picked each flower, ran back and stuffed another stem into her hand.

A sudden sweet remembrance brought to mind the tenderness of the man she would marry tomorrow and who shyly expressed his love in so many endearing ways. Lily raised her face and heart toward heaven. *Heavenly Father, I'm just learning about You. I want to be a good wife and mother to Tex and Genevieve and the boys. Allena and Mary Lou tell me that You want the best for Your children no matter who they are or how they may have sinned and that's why Jesus died on the cross. Thank You for a good man to care for me and my children. Help us to also give him the love he needs and deserves for marrying us.* Lily looked toward heaven. *But dear God, You'll have to show me how.* Lily wiped her eyes and bowed her head in silence for a moment. *Thank You, Jesus, Amen.*

A sweet peace of acceptance and love soothed the trembling beat of her heart. She opened her eyes. A feeling of peace spread all through her. She glanced around for her daughter, who was nowhere in sight.

Suddenly a mop of curls popped up from the center of a bevy of Texas bluebonnets.

Lily motioned Genevieve to come.

Hair and blossoms flying Genevieve came running to her mother.

Lily stooped, laid her bouquet on the ground, and spread her arms. Genevieve, tinkling with childish laughter, a spindly bouquet squeezed in her tiny fist, sprayed a trail of escaped flowers as she ran laughing into her mother's arms.

Lily held her close. The Bible verse Allena had read that morning during devotions spoke within: "My cup runneth over." Tears coarsed down Lily's cheeks, tears for happiness she never knew existed. Her cup was running over.

Genevieve backed away, concerned. "Mama cry?"

Lily cupped her child's concerned face. "Something else you'll learn someday, my child. There are tears of hurt and tears of happiness. Grandma calls them happy tears." She smiled broadly as her daughter's troubled face brightened.

Genevieve laughed, "Hap-py tears, hap-py tears."

Lily kissed her daughter's cheek and took her hand. "I think we have enough flowers, don't you? Let's go home and give some to Grandma."

Genevieve grabbed her mother's outstretched hand and pulled her in the direction of the ranch house.

On the ranch porch Allena stood, her hand shading her eyes as two small bouncing dots gradually grew into Lily and Genevieve. They were coming. All was ready for Lily's wedding tomorrow. Only a few burlap bags, baskets, and wooden boxes containing the last of Lily's and Genevieve's belongings stood waiting on the porch for transport. This morning Lars and Wilmot's last belongings had been taken by Tex up to their new cabin. Lily's wedding dress hung on a hook in Allena's bedroom, not to be seen until she wore it.

Watching them come, an unwelcome sadness clutched Allena's heart. After Tex and Lily's honeymoon she would lose four members of her family from under her roof. She would miss the children. But there were still six left at the main ranch, she, Nelson and Laura, Zack, little Zachary, and Hattie.

Allena smiled. But not for long. She clasped her arms around her middle as if to hold and nurture the special secret Nelson and Laura had been unable to keep so decided to tell only her. She had felt honored, included. They had sworn her to secrecy then told her of the precious child Laura carried within her. They had wanted to keep it to themselves until after Lily's wedding to make the announcement a special moment for the family as well as for them.

Allena had been ecstatic with the news and daily praised God and prayed for a healthy child to be born with two good legs and a strong body. She fought herself to keep from returning to the memories of the years of working with Nelson's legs.

Periodically, when fear swamped her, she immediately prayed to a Father God she knew could deliver a strong, healthy child to Nelson and Laura. Allena asked forgiveness for her weak faith and leaned heavily on her Lord for belief that it could be so.

When she walked back into the house it seemed strangely quiet. *Life keeps alive with each generation.* The words reverberated in the room. Allena swung around almost expecting to see her husband, Zachary, standing at the door. He used to say that. Her heart pounded with the words.

Allena closed her eyes and pictured her husband, tall, stately, handsome, his penetrating eyes searching her very being. "Yes, Zachary," she answered aloud. "Just as our children replace us." She pursed her lips and tried to suppress a sudden rush of tears, but they had a mind of their own and cascaded over her cheeks. "Oh my dear husband, I miss you so." She drew her handkerchief from her apron pocket, quickly daubed away her tears, and stood smiling as Lily and Genevieve walked into the ranch yard with their arms full of flowers.

Genevieve skipped ahead and ran toward her grandmother with a fist full of flowers valiantly struggling to hold up their drooping heads. Her little brows frowned when she saw her Grandma wiping her eyes. Her little face showed concern. "Gramma cry?"

Allena spread a smile across her face. "I'm so happy to see you I am crying happy tears."

"Gamma cry hap-py tears!" she called back to her mother. Lily smiled and entered the gate, a large basket of flowers in each hand. As much as she loved this ranch she was anxious for the time when she, Tex, Lars, Wilmot, and Genevieve would all be neatly settled in their new home, a dream Lily had never dared dream before. For the first time, she thanked God for Doug. Without her realizing it, God had used him to help her dreams come true. Now Tex in his shy, awkward way loved her with a kind of love she never knew existed. Lily felt clean and pure for the first time in her life. She now understood Mary Lou's favorite hymn, "God works in mysterious ways His wonders to perform."

The heavenly Father's current wonders in Lily's life had released a new sense of peace and meaning for Lily. It settled over her like a warm, comforting blanket.

seven

The morning sun crept through the window and kissed Lily Langdon's eyelids to announce her special day. They raised slowly, drowsily, then opened wide.

My wedding day!

She glanced at her sleeping daughter, quietly folded back the covers so as not to wake Genevieve, slowly slid her bare feet to the floor, and stood up.

Genevieve didn't move.

Lily dressed quickly, slipped out of the room, and hurried to the kitchen.

Allena glanced up from her bowl of oatmeal and smiled. "Good morning, Lily. Happy is the bride the sun shines on, and it's shining brightly today! How'd you sleep?" She patted the chair next to hers. "Come, sit here so Hattie and I can fuss a bit over the bride."

Lily leaned and planted a kiss on Allena's cheek, much to Allena's surprise, then slid onto her chair. "Believe it or not, I had a good night's sleep. All I had to do was lay my head on the pillow! Even Genevieve slept quiet as a mouse all night. Probably exhausted after our running all over yesterday picking flowers!"

Allena nodded. "I remember one time I complained to my mother about being tired and about having to work all the time. Her crisp comment was 'I think God planned it that way, otherwise we'd all be lazier than sin.'"

"Here we are," Hattie hustled from the stove with two breakfast plates, placed one each in front of Allena and

49

Lily, hurried back for her own plate, and took her place.

The three women bowed their heads.

"Good morning, Father," Allena began. "We thank You for this new day and ask Your special blessing upon Lily and Tex as You join them together today as man and wife. We all rejoice with them. Thank You for Your constant provision for our needs and ask Your blessing upon us. In Jesus' name, Amen."

The women ate slowly with none of the usual chatter. They had worked very hard all week to get to this point and relaxed over their breakfast in the assurance they had done their task well.

Allena looked up at Lily. "Do you have any idea how much we are all going to miss you and the children living here?"

Lily laughed. "I should think you would be glad for a breather! It isn't as if we're moving far away. We're about the same distance as Tom and Mary Lou." Lily laughed again. "Don't worry Mother, I think Laura and Nelson being here will keep things stirred up. Especially Laura. She has enough ideas and energy to keep everything and everyone going around in circles."

Allena nodded and laughed. "That she has! Always been that way." Allena harkened back to shortly after she and her husband had purchased the Circle Z, a pretty little eight-year-old neighbor girl began riding her horse to the Circle Z on any pretense. It wasn't long before Allena was enjoying her young visitor and indulged herself by pretending Laura was her own. Now Laura was married to one of her sons. Allena had learned early in life that the Lord always has His own special way of answering His children's prayers.

The women ate quietly, savoring a few rare moments of peace and quiet before everything broke loose.

Lily wasn't the least bit hungry and picked at her breakfast in fear of disturbing the butterflies in her stomach.

Hattie, first one done, began clearing up. "Jess 'n the cowboys have had the beeves strung up over the fire since way before daylight. I could smell them early this mornin'. They should be just right by noon. They got them tables all set up in nothin' flat in the ranch yard." Hattie carried dishes to the drainboard and peered out the window. "Looks like the good Lord is going to bless the weddin' with a nice day." Hattie smiled. "In town, yesterday, people were talkin' about the weddin'. From what I hear everybody's lookin' forward to it and said they're comin'."

Lily smiled. "They're very kind. Ruthella sent word with one of the cowboys yesterday that since she lives so close to the church she'll pick some wildflowers and take them to the church early this morning and make sure everything is ready so we won't have to get to the church till half an hour before the wedding. If we leave here at ten that should be enough time, don't you think?"

"Plenty," Allena answered and couldn't contain her smile. She had never seen Lily so nervous or talkative. She thought back to the first time she met Lily, the day Doug brought her home as his bride. How outraged she had been at her son for stooping to marry one of those shameful saloon girls and bringing such disgrace on his family.

Allena now gazed at the lovely young woman beside her. She bore little resemblence to the woman Doug brought home that day. *Why is it we are always surprised at what God can do in the life of one of His children?* He had known Lily's true heart from her beginning and in His mercy had made a way, even through a wayward son, to give her the opportunity to escape her life of sin. A humbling thought settled. *God does that for all of us if we let Him.*

After a hurried breakfast the three women brought out their week's work of food preparation, all ready for the planned feast after the wedding. The pungent odor of roast beef began to permeate the air. Pans of fruited wedding cake stood covered on the sideboard. Sawhorses and board tables had been set up in the yard and were covered with white sheets, waiting to hold the special gifts of food brought by neighbors and friends. Every woman in each family would share the best from her kitchen.

After a slow start the early morning hours flew by; then it was suddenly time to get ready for church.

Lily went to her room to dress. Her hands shook as she donned her stockings, white drawers, and chemise, swung her petticoat and long, blue skirt over her head, buttoned them at the waist and straightened the draped folds in the front of her overskirt. It curved gracefully over her hips. Her white basque had soft lace around the high neck collar with matching lace on the cuffs. She, Hattie, and Allena had worked long hours. They had sent through the mail for sewing patterns from the Butterick Publishing Company in New York. It was the first time they had ever worked with a store-boughten ready-made pattern. The tissue-paper pattern had been folded in an instruction sheet that even showed how to lay the pattern on the material. It had been a great help, and the women decided they would send for other style patterns in their sizes. The cutting and sewing had been much easier than to mold the cloth over the body to cut it to size or to use another dress for a pattern, as they usually did. All three women were pleased at the fine style and fit of the finished dress.

Lily had just slipped the last shell hairpin into her thick chestnut bun, piled high on top of her head, when Mary Lou walked into the room with a wreath of flowers she had made.

"Here, I thought this would look right pretty around your bun."

Lily watched in the mirror as Mary Lou placed it on her head like a crown.

Allena smiled, clasped her hands together, and nodded. "Lily! You are a beautiful bride! Tex is a lucky man."

Lily's eyes filled with tears and she lowered her head. She had always denied herself the luxury of crying, but determine as she would, her eyes took on a mind of their own, spilling tears in profusion over her cheeks and leaving sprays of damp spots on her wedding dress.

Allena gently folded Lily into her arms. "Cry, Lily, and wash all your former hurts away till you remember them no more. Praise God! He is giving you a chance to be the woman He made you to be."

At ten-thirty, the three women were ready and waiting when Tom and the children drove into the yard in the wagon to pick up Mary Lou and Hattie and take them to church.

Right behind them came Tex, driving a surrey borrowed from a neighbor. He was all dressed up in a brand new pair of black pants, a fancy cowboy shirt, string tie, a shiny new pair of cowboy boots, and his Stetson tipped slightly over one ear.

Tom raised his eyebrows and grinned.

That grin turned Tex's face beet red.

Typical nervous bridegroom, Tom thought. He remembered when. . .

Tex helped Lily into the backseat of the surrey. His

eyes brushed past hers like a scared rabbit.

Lily's heart lifted a prayer of thanks to God for His gift of love to her in this shy cowboy who would soon be her husband. He hustled to the other side of the surrey to assist Allena into the seat beside her.

Lily and Allena's eyes met. Allena reached over and patted Lily's hand for reassurance. To Lily it was a steadying touch of love and acceptance.

The morning sun spread its soft, gentle rays of warm blessing on everyone as the carriages hurried along the road. When they turned into the churchyard it was already more than half filled with horses, buggies and wagons of smiling neighbors all dressed in their Sunday best. A wedding was a big event in any community. It enabled everyone to take a breather from endless work, giving respite from thankless tasks that never seemed ended and the opportunity to socialize with their friends and neighbors.

Tom pulled his wagon around to the side of the church. Tex followed.

Ruthella, all smiles, hurried to meet the bride and groom. "Everything is ready," she assured them and turned to Mary Lou. "Your seats are all up front in your usual place."

Another buggy turned into the churchyard. It was the Reverend Milfield, the only clergy in the area who could marry them legally. Otherwise they would have had to be married by a judge. After Lily's experience with Doug and a judge, she had made only one request—to be married by a minister. She was now a Christian and had felt it only proper.

Reverend Milfield bowed politely to the ladies then asked to speak to the bridegroom. Tex, Tom, and the Reverend stepped off to the side and talked a few minutes.

Tex nodded his head several times, then Tom walked over, spoke a word to Lily, then went into the church and took his seat next to Mary Lou and his mother on the family bench.

The Reverend took his place.

Finally, the organ pealed a few strong chords and Ruthella moved in to the familiar strains of the wedding march. At the back of the church Lily looked up at Tex and drank in the reassuring caress of love from his warm eyes. He offered her his arm, and they walked down the aisle together and stood before the minister.

The Reverend Milfield began in ponderous tones, "Dearly Beloved, we are assembled here in the presence of God to join this man and this woman in holy marriage which is instituted of God, regulated by His commandments, blessed by our Lord Jesus Christ and to be held in honor among all men. Let us, therefore, reverently remember that God has established and sanctified marriage for the welfare and happiness of mankind.

Our Savior has declared that a man shall forsake his father and mother and cleve unto his wife. He has instructed those who enter into this relationship to cherish a mutual esteem and love; to bear with each other's infirmities and weaknesses; to comfort each other in sickness, trouble and sorrow; in honesty and industry to provide for each other and for their household in temporal things; to pray for and encourage each other in the things which pertain to God; and to live together as heirs of the grace of life."

The Reverend turned to Tex and Lily. "Forasmuch as you have come hither to be made one in this blessed estate, I charge you both, that if either of you know any reason—" the minister then looked out upon the assembly, "or anyone know why you may not rightly be joined together in marriage, you now acknowledge it. Be well assured that if any persons are joined together otherwise than as God's Word allows, their union is not blessed by Him."

The Reverent Milfield paused and his penetrating eyes slowly moved across the assembly. Even the air seemed to hold its breath. He turned to Tex. "Theodore Williams, wilt thou have this woman to be thy wife and wilt thou pledge thy troth to her in all love and honor, duty and service and all faith and tenderness, to live with her and cherish her, according to the ordinance of God in the holy bond of marriage?"

Tex cleared his throat. His "I do" came out strong and clear.

The Reverend turned to Lily. "Lillian Langdon, wilt thou have this man to be thy husband and wilt thou pledge thy troth to him in all love and honor, in all duty and service, in all faith and tenderness to live with him and cherish him according to the ordinance of God in the holy bond of marriage?"

"I will," Lily answered.

Mary Lou's thoughts carried her back to her own wedding. How, lovely God had brought about the fulfillment of her lifelong dream—to be a rancher's wife—Tom's wife.

Now their heavenly Father was answering Lily's dream of a life with a good husband, children, and a home for all of them. Mary Lou bowed her head in grateful thanks for God's special care of each one of His children.

". . .we are gathered here to join together this man and this woman into the state of holy matrimony. Marriage is a holy estate ordained by God our Heavenly Father and is not be be entered into lightly.

"Who giveth this woman to this man?"

A pregnant hush fell over the congregation.

No one had thought of that.

"I do." The voice was the strong, determined voice of Allena.

Necks craned and a hushed buzz rumbled the room. Reverend Milfield jolted to attention, met Allena's determined gaze, nodded and continued.

He turned to Tex. "Do you Theodore Williams take this woman, Lillian Langdon, to be your lawful wedded wife, to honor, cherish, protect, love her and keep yourself only unto her until death you do part?"

Tex cleared his throat and swallowed. "I do."

The Reverend turned to Lily. "Lillian Langdon, do you take Theodore Williams to be your lawfully wedded husband, to love, honor, obey and keep yourself only unto him until death you do part?"

Lily faced Tex, smiled and spoke from her heart. "I do."

The Reverend turned to Tex. "What token do you offer this woman of the sincerity of your intentions?"

Tex fumbled in the breast pocket of his vest, brought forth a plain gold ring and placed it in the Reverend's outstretched hand. He returned it to Tex.

Tex took Lily's hand and looked into her eyes.

"Repeat after me. With this ring I thee wed—"

"With this ring I thee wed—"

Tex slid the ring on her finger, looked up, and poured love from his eyes into hers.

Mary Lou daubed her eyes, reliving each word of the ceremony.

"Now by the power vested in me, I do pronounce this man and this woman to be husband and wife until death do they part. May our Father God bless this union with His grace and mercy."

The Reverend bowed his head. "Let us pray. Our Father God, you ordained from the creation of this world that man and woman should live in companionship. We now ask Thy holy blessing upon this new union and ask You to guide them to live within Your will and so honor Jesus Christ, our Savior. We pray in the name of the Father, the Son and the Holy Spirit. Amen."

Reverend Milfield looked up at the young man and woman before him and smiled. "I now pronounce you man and wife together. May God bless you." The Reverend glanced at Tex and grinned. "You may kiss your bride now, son."

Tex turned, put his arms around Lily and kissed her tenderly. They turned and faced a roomful of smiling friends. Tex took Lily's hand and they walked back up the aisle while the organ pumped out "Blest Be the Tie that Binds." They were greeted outside the church by the Circle Z cowboys, who whisked them away.

Inside, Reverend Milfield raised his hand and spoke to the congregation of family and friends. "I have been asked by the Langdon family to invite you all to the Circle Z ranch for the wedding feast."

Smiles broke across faces and the room came alive.

The churchyard emptied quickly. Guests loaded themselves into their own buggies and wagons or mounted their horses and followed the newlyweds' surrey to the Circle Z. Everyone was hungry.

eight

Shortly after one o'clock, horses, buggies, wagons, and carriages of all kinds streamed into the Circle Z lane and parked anywhere they could find a space. People flowed out of them to join the celebration of Lily and Tex's wedding. The titillating aroma of roasted beeves greeted them and whetted everyone's appetite.

Each woman carried a dish, a pan, or a basket containing her family's special contribution to the wedding feast. Before long the tables were groaning.

When Reverend Milfield arrived, he moved and chatted among the guests and invited all to come to church. Finally when given the signal, he held up his hand until he got everyone's attention. "Let's ask God's blessing on this special meal." He bowed his head.

A hush descended as all heads bowed. Reverend Milfield called for the grace and blessing of God on the bride and groom, their family, friends and food. His "Amen" drew forth echoes from the bowed heads of the men standing round; then everyone shuffled to the table to find a seat of some kind and began passing their plates. Women filled plates with what was before them and passed them on until everyone was served.

While they were eating, Skinny Adams arrived all dressed up in his big Stetson and fancy shirt, his fiddle tucked under his arm and gladly accepted the invitation to join the guests for dinner.

Get-togethers of all the neighbors usually happened only at special times like weddings, funerals, harvesting, and barn dances and gave welcome respite from the harsh labors of every day. The women, in particular, enjoyed the company of other womenfolk. Their days were often spent in long, lonely hours and doubly hard work when the men were away on cattle drives or riding the range. It was only at church, weddings, harvest time, quilting parties, or a barn dance they saw much of one another. They relished the rest, the ample variety of food on the table, and the opportunity to talk to other women as the older children played and cared for the younger ones.

Men seized the opportunity to discuss and compare crop prices, trade, new improvements made on each farm or ranch, and add their appraisal of the new combine harvester that was making the strenuous work of harvesting a great deal easier.

As soon as Skinny Adams had eaten his fill, he cradled his fiddle under his chin and moved slowly around, softly playing the well-known Civil War love song "Lorena." Everyone joined in singing. He moved into "I'll Take You Home Again, Kathleen" and "My Darling Clementine." When the meal was over, his bow suddenly came alive and bounced into "Goober Peas." That set everyone's feet tapping, and he headed for the barn.

Tom grabbed Mary Lou's hand. They seized the hands of the bride and groom and called, "Everybody out to the barn so we can celebrate with our feet!"

Skinny began playing waltzes as soon as he reached the barn. One by one, the male guests now had the opportunity to take a turn or two with the bride long enough to pin greenbacks to her dress.

Suddenly Skinny picked up the tempo and called, "Ladies in the center, gents round them run, swing yer rope, cowboy, an' git yo' one."

Soon feet were stomping and skirts a-twirling as the

fiddle enticed everyone into action. The young children held hands, jumped, skipped, and twirled. The older girls waited eagerly to be chosen.

Suddenly the music stopped and Skinny called out to the men, "Now take your pretty partner and we'll have a quadrille!"

Squares were quickly formed.

The fiddle squeaked out "Turkey in the Straw," and soon the barn echoed the rhythmic shuffling of feet as the ladies' skirts swirled high and low through set after set, call after call. Dancing was a favorite pastime of most of the pioneers.

Then came the call "Swing the other gal, now swing yer sweet. Paw dirt, doggies, stomp your feet. Swing and march—first couple lead—clear around the hall an' then stampede."

The "stampede" headed for the pump, where men wet the ladies' handkerchiefs. The women thankfully daubed their warm faces, neck and wrists. The men splashed their faces, some even stuck their whole heads or hair under the water to cool down. They shook the water off like sheepdogs then led their partners to tables filled with pitchers of water and lemonade, cold tea, and delicious baked goods from the ladies.

Finally, Tex grabbed Lily's elbow. "Come on, let's go," he said quietly and guided her toward the house. With everyone busy, they thought they might be able to sneak out without being seen.

But Mary Lou saw them leave and followed. When she walked into Lily's room, Lily was frantically trying to manage buttons with shaking hands. "Let me help you, Lily," she said. In short order, Lily was securely buttoned into her travel dress and ready to go.

Lily stood for a moment looking at Mary Lou then

smiled, walked to her, and put her arms around her. She didn't speak, just clung.

Mary Lou felt her pounding heart, pushed Lily back, and gazed into her swimming eyes. This was a new Lily, the shy bride she had never been allowed to be. Mary Lou cupped her face with her hands. "You're going to be fine, Lily. Tex is going to make you a fine husband."

Lily nodded and smiled. "I know." She dipped her head for a moment then looked into Mary Lou's eyes. "This may sound like a funny thing, coming from me, but this the first time I have ever had the choice of giving myself to a man who loves me."

The words pierced Mary Lou's heart. She thought of Doug and cupped Lily's face in her hands. "That's all past, Lily, forget it. You're not that woman now. You are God's forgiven child, Tex's wife. He and your husband will watch over you. You don't have to be afraid anymore. All you have to do is love them both." Mary Lou suddenly grinned. "I discovered my main duty was to love, be a helpmate and companion to my husband, love and care for our children and be a good neighbor. If I'm doing all those the best I can, God will honor me."

Mary Lou reached into her pocket, withdrew a handkerchief, daubed Lily's swimming eyes, then grabbed her hand. "Come. Knowing husbands, yours is probably impatiently waiting for you and wondering why you are taking so long to get dressed. Men never seem to understand we are just trying to look pretty for them!" Mary Lou pushed Lily at arm's length. "And you look beautiful." She planted a kiss on Lily's cheek, and they walked to the door just as Allena came in.

Allena stood for a moment, studied Lily, then spread her arms.

Lily walked into them.

Life would change for all of them. Enough words had been said. Allena just held Lily, kissed her on the forehead, and released her. "God bless you, my dear daughter. The Lord go with you."

Lily's eyes welled with tears. "Thank you—Mother."

Allena touched Lily's cheek and smiled. "May the good Lord bless you, child."

Lily nodded and hurried outside.

Tex stood by the surrey, fidgeting with the lines and darting nervous, anxious glances at the door. When Lily appeared, he jumped to the ground to help Lily into the surrey.

Smiling guests had come from the barn and circled round, waiting to wave them off. Standing beside Allena were Lily's children. Lily gathered the bubbly little Genevieve into her arms and smothered her with loving kisses. "Be a sweetheart for Grandma. I love you so much." Genevieve patted the tears slipping down her mother's cheeks. As Lily handed her baby girl to Allena, she saw that Lars and Wilmot's eyes displayed fear and confusion.

Lily dropped to her knees, circled them in her arms, and kissed each one on the cheek. "Tex and I will be back in a couple days; then we all will go back to our new house. You get your things all ready." She wiped Wilmot's tears and smiled at Lars, who was standing very straight with his protective arm around his little brother, fighting to keep his lower lip from trembling.

Lily kissed them both. "We aren't leaving you. You'll be fine with your—" Lily looked up at Allena and smiled, "with your grandma. When we come back, Tex will be your papa, and we'll all go home to live in our new house." Lily stood, kissed each boy's forehead, climbed into the surrey, and blew them a kiss.

Allena moved behind the boys and put her arms around them. Then the bride and groom were off amid waves and good wishes for happiness and a shower of rice from their neighbors to wish them prosperity.

The wagon rumbled down the ranch lane and turned onto the road toward town. Lily waved and they were gone.

Slowly, neighbors, one by one gathered their children and food dishes and headed for their own homes. It was chore time.

Mary Lou watched the last one go, dropped on the nearest bench, and cried.

Tom was at her side immediately. "What's wrong?"

Mary Lou looked at her husband through a veil of tears, reached into her pocket for her hanky, and mopped her tears. "I'm just so happy for Lily and Tex."

Tom grinned and teased, "I thought when you're happy you were supposed to smile!"

She stood up and slid into his waiting arms. "I know, but sometimes when you're the happiest the tears insist on coming."

Tom looked down into her face, grinned, and shook his head. "I don't think we men will ever understand women."

Mary Lou batted her tears with her eyelashes and laughed. "You're not supposed to. That's what makes us so intriguing!"

Tom pulled her back into his arms. "I'm sure the good Lord knew what he was doing, but you ladies sure gives us fellas a pause sometimes."

Mary Lou tweaked his nose. "Well, we have to get your attention some way!"

Tom put his arm around her, and laughing, they joined the others in the cleanup.

nine

Mary Lou stepped out her ranch door, took a deep breath of the fresh morning air, and basked in the warm sunshine. A sudden flurry of activity at the main ranch captured her attention. A rider galloped hard toward their barn, halted in a cloud of dust, and called for Tom. It was Laura. She quickly dismounted at the barn door and hurried in.

Mary Lou shaded her eyes. Had something happened? She waited a long moment then decided to walk to the barn. Halfway there, Tom suddenly emerged from the barn, riding Tinder bareback, and galloped hard toward the main ranch.

Tommy ran after his father then stopped. With a frown on his face he turned and followed Laura and his sister as they walked toward his mother.

"What happened?" Mary Lou called out as they neared her. The serious expression on Laura's face brought fear to her heart. Something terrible must have happened.

"We just received a telegraph message from Darcy's father," she gasped between breaths. "Darcy has been in an accident. She was thrown from her horse and is calling for Zack. I guess she's hurt real bad. Her father asked Zack to come immediately and bring Baby Zack with him. Unfortunately, Zack left this morning on the train for the Texas State Legislature. The operator telegraphed back to Darcy's family that as soon as they locate Zack they will have him contact his father-in-law." Laura lowered her head and said softly, "As much as I had a hard time with Darcy, I pray her injuries aren't serious."

Mary Lou nodded in prayerful agreement. She called the twins and sat them together on Laura's horse, and they walked fast to the the main ranch.

Hattie and Allena had just finished breakfast cleanup when they entered the ranch kitchen. The twins raced toward Baby Zack and Genevieve.

As the women talked, Mary Lou's tender heart reached for Darcy. Her confidence in God still encouraged her to hold to the belief that Darcy could have been reached if she had just stayed in Texas longer and tried a little harder to adjust.

"God never gives up on anyone," Mama had often said, "and we shouldn't either." For all Darcy's scornful, tempestuous ways that had driven everyone to distraction, Mary Lou had felt a kinship—perhaps because they had both been new brides in the family. She was sorry she had not tried harder to befriend Darcy to help her make the adjustment of the abrupt change to ranch life. Because Mary Lou had grown up on a ranch, much was familiar to her, but she now realized that for Darcy it must have been like a foreign land with none of the niceties of Boston that she was accustomed to. Yet, perhaps this accident would lay her down long enough to think about what she really wanted, her husband and son or Boston's high society.

Mary Lou remembered Mama saying, "Sometimes God has to set us down hard to get our attention." Mary Lou smiled. *Just as I have to do with Tommy and Beth once in a while.* "I do hope Darcy isn't hurt too bad," she said.

Lily shook her head. "The telegram said 'serious'."

Somehow the news had spread to their neighbors. Just before noon Emily Shepard walked into the kitchen and placed two large baskets filled with bread and meat on the kitchen table. She was followed by her sons Matthew, Mark, Luke, and John, who carried in baskets and pans, set them on the table, grinned, and hurried outside to join the men.

Emily walked over to Allena, looked lovingly into her eyes, and patted her shoulder. "When trouble comes, friends need to share the bad as well as the good."

Looks of loving concern passed between the two women as they readied the table. When the coffee and tea were steaming, everyone sat down. Prayers for Zack, Darcy, and her family were expressed along with thanks for the food.

The presence of dear friends and neighbors eased the tension that had held everyone in its iron grip since the news of Darcy had arrived.

In Harness, at the train station, Tom and Nelson sat enthralled as they watched the telegraph in action. What an invention! Imagine! Messages sent from one place to another on pieces of wire! It boggled Tom's mind. What a help it was to communicate between towns. Between towns? Between states! The message to Zack had been sent all the way from Boston!

"It's a miracle, that's what it is." Tom said to Jim Johnson, the telegrapher. "Imagine, being able to send words halfway across the country on wire and get an answer the same day! Why, it would have taken weeks to get a message to Zack by stagecoach or even the old pony express."

Jim smiled. "Yep! And have you seen them new phonographs? Tom Edison invented them. It has a flat wheel that goes around and you put these black flat plates that has grooves cut out in them—they call 'em records. Then there's a swing arm with a needle in it that you put in the grooves on the outside edge of the record. Then you start the thing spinnin', and it plays music or talkin'." He laughed. "I'd like to get me one of those someday. Hey! ain't this a great time to be livin'!"

It took two long hours before the telegraph clicked a message from Zack that he was on his way home by train. Tom and Nelson headed for the Circle Z.

The family was in the middle of making hurried plans for Zack's trip to Boston.

Allena had folded Zack a couple extra clean shirts and packed more underwear and socks to add to what he had taken with him to Texas. As she worked, she grew more uneasy and finally expressed her concern to the family. "It will be very difficult for both Zack and Baby Zack to travel all that way. What about food and someplace to sleep?"

"You just sleep on the train, Mother, in your seat." Nelson answered.

Allena shook her head. "Why they will have to sleep sitting up on the train all night! I should go and help care for Baby Zack." The words were no more out of her mouth then Allena looked over at Laura, who was large with child. She could be due next week or before the month was out. Allena had planned to deliver the baby. . . and check it. . . She didn't want Nelson or Laura to know how concerned she was, but she figured they were both thinking the same as she but hadn't made any mention of it. Would Nelson's child be whole, hardy and able to walk? Her concerned thoughts spilled out. "I would go and take care of Baby Zack but—Laura's baby could be born while I am gone and I. . .and. . .Laura had expressly asked me to be with her to birth and inspect the baby." The thought of Nelson's child inheriting his weakness was never voiced, but fear lodged in the house unspoken, and Allena wanted to be there just in case. Early massage and care were especially vital immediately after birth.

During the discussion, Hattie spoke up and flatly stated, "I could go with Zack and take care of Baby Zack."

Her words hung in the air for consideration by surprised family members.

"Oh, Hattie," Allena commented, "that would be a hard trip for you with Baby Zack."

Hattie shook her head and laughed. "It would be like a vacation compared to one day's work around here! Anyway, I've never been on a train."

Eyes moved from one to another as the family digested the idea.

"Well, Hattie," Allena finally said. "Then let's sort of gather you together just in case. Then we'll see what Zack wants to do when he gets here."

"I think we ought to meet Zack at the train in Harness," Tom said. "He needs to go as soon as he can if Darcy is hurt as bad as we've been told. He could save a day's ride if we were there to meet him, and he could board the next train going east right away."

The family looked at one another. It made sense.

The women scurried to pack for Hattie and Baby Zack. Tom and Nelson packed what they thought Zack might need for the longer trip.

Finally, all was ready. The whole family climbed into buggies and wagons and drove to the railroad station on the outskirts of Harness to meet the train.

Zack was the first one to swing off the train and spied his family waiting for him. His concerned face widened with a grateful grin.

Allena threw her arms around her tall, distinguished

son, then backed away and let him and Tom talk. She walked to Hattie, who stood in the midst of their baggage, all dressed for traveling awaiting the final decision. Allena reached forward and placed an envelope in Hattie's hand. "I want you to give this to Mrs. Whitney. It's a letter to her as one mother to another and a written prayer that has helped me in my times of trial. I don't know whether she is a Christian or not, but prayers help everybody. Somehow I don't think she will be offended. Zack said she is a sweet, gracious lady."

Hattie nodded and tucked the envelope into her purse and gave it a pat. "Just from things Zack has said I think I'm going to like that lady."

Zack was outwardly pleased with the arrangements to take Baby Zack with him, doubly pleased that Hattie would go as nursemaid. On the trip home, his legal mind had searched some of the ramifications that might enter into his father-in-law's cagey, legal, maneuvering mind. Zack didn't trust him. He would have preferred to go alone if he hadn't felt it only right to try to let his son see his mother again. Could it be that in her weakness she might discover the joy of having a son? Stranger things had happened. Circumstances change people. His mother had firmly embedded in each one of her boy's hearts and minds that God never runs out of miracles and that Jesus has already paid for everybody's sins on the cross.

So regardless of what his father-in-law thought, Zack felt he was doing the right thing. *If Darcy is as injured as they said in the telegram. . .maybe. . .yet. . .* He'd wait to make any judgments till he got there.

The train going east huffed and puffed into the station and released hugh white clouds of steam as it wheezed to a stop.

Amid farewell kisses and hugs, Zack, carrying his son, helped Hattie up the train steps, found some seats, piled their luggage under the seat, sat down, and leaned to the window to wave just as the train began pulling away from the station. His whole family stood outside waving and smiling. Their active, concerned love tugged at his heart. He was proud to be a Langdon.

Hattie settled in her seat, straightened her skirt, took off her Sunday church-meetin' hat, then reached for Baby Zack.

Zack grinned. "Hattie, you just sit back and enjoy the scenery for a while. I'll hold him." He perched his son on his knee and smiled into the child's upturned face.

Wide-eyed, Baby Zack suddenly nestled into the safety of his father's arms and stared up with questioning eyes.

Never in all his growing years had Zack appreciated the meaning of family as he had today. He remembered his strong, steady father and for the first time in a long time felt a hollow ache and a longing for his father's presence. He had automatically become the head of the family since he was the oldest son and a lawyer. His chest rose and fell in a deep sigh. He felt as if he could use a big dose of his father's wisdom right now.

Zack was thankful he had been able to delegate most of the decisions about the ranch into Tom and Nelson's capable hands. When he had left for the East to study law, he had been rather reluctant to turn the office books and keys over to Doug, but being second son in line it was his responsibility. He hadn't trusted Doug then but prayed and hoped Doug would measure up. Now with Doug gone, he had been able to turn complete management of the ranch over to his two younger brothers which freed him to pursue his own law business.

Zack glanced over at Hattie and grinned. She sat

ramrod straight, chin up, gazing out the window, her face filled with delight. Zack grinned at her obvious pleasure. He fondly remembered the first day she came to the ranch. He had been eight, Doug six, Tom four, and Nelson just a baby. His mother had found her in Harness when her landlord was evicting her for not having paid her rent, so Allena paid her rent, packed her up, and brought her home to help in the kitchen at the ranch. Hattie became second mother to all of them and had been a stalwart sustaining comfort to his mother since the tragedy of his father's death.

A fresh discovery perched in Zack's mind. *Fancy clothes and prestige never make a lady. It begins in her heart and grows by loving.* He had learned that from his mother. Zack caught Hattie's eye and smiled at her.

She returned his smile. The delighted expression on her face told him she was having the time of·her life. He was doubly thankful to her for coming with him. Baby Zack was used to her and obeyed her well. He wasn't surprised. As a young boy he remembered she had never said anything twice. If any of them hadn't "listened up," they were left out. Zack grinned. Yep. It was about time Hattie had a vacation. He settled back for the long trip.

Three days later, after changing trains twice as they crossed the mid-eastern states the engine huffed and puffed its way into Boston and wheezed a sigh of relief.

So did Hattie. Though she had been fascinated watching the country fly by, her bones felt as if every one had been hammered numb. She was already looking forward to a night's rest, laid out flat on a solid bed.

Zack glanced down at his son's sleepy, dreamy eyes staring up at him. He smiled and touched the tip of Baby Zack's nose with his finger. "We're going to see your mama, son."

ten

The train slowed to a stop at the Boston station. Zack rose, allowed Hattie and Baby Zack to move into the aisle, and retrieved the baggage from under the seat.

Hattie flopped the handle of her pocketbook over her arm, took Baby Zack's hand, and followed Zack quickly to the end of the car.

Zack hopped to the platform, lifted his son to the ground, and grabbed Hattie's outstretched hand as she stepped from the train to the platform. Zack motioned to a waiting cabbie and helped Hattie into it.

The horses stepped high as they rode through Boston on the cobblestone streets. Hattie's eyes widened at the parade of grand buggies with fancy dressed men and beautiful women in large plumed hats that rode past them. "My, my! This is a big, grand place."

"Yes it is," Zack answered. In a momentary flash he viewed it fresh through Hattie's eyes, with new understanding of how Darcy must see Texas. Even though the new house he was building in Texas was elegant in its own way, it still smacked of Texas. Boston was a lot more civilized and cultured and still was "home" for Darcy because home is where your heart is. His wife had painfully taught him that.

All the time he had been in Boston studying to become a lawyer he remembered that periodically his mind and heart longed for the wide open spaces of Texas. At first he had been delighted he had escaped to the East to pursue his dream to be a lawyer, but as he neared the end of his studies, he had found himself longing for the wide open spaces of Texas where a constant wind blew. Summers were often oppressively hot in Boston.

The carriage finally turned and moved through wide wrought-iron gates and deposited its passengers at the front door of an elegant Tudor mansion. Hattie gratefully clasped the hand of the chauffeur as he helped her and Baby Zack alight.

Zack paid the driver, picked up his son, walked up on the porch, and turned the handle of the doorbell.

The front door opened slowly, then Emery, the butler, smiled in recognition and swung the door wide. "Mr. Langdon! Good to see you, sir." He stepped aside as Hattie and Baby Zack entered. "We're mighty glad you're here, sir." A wan smile crossed his mouth then his face resumed its dutiful mask. He carried in their luggage and placed it against the hall wall and nodded to Zack. "Hope you had a good trip, sir."

"Yes, we did, thank you." Zack stopped and turned to Hattie. "Emery, this is Hattie Benson and my son, Baby Zack."

Emery smiled at Hattie and placed his hand on the boy's head. "What a fine big boy you are. I'm glad to meet you, sir. Your mama has talked a lot about you."

Hattie tried to keep her face composed. Her thoughts went askance at Darcy's concern. She had seemed to find him a hindrance when she was in Texas. Other than playing with him now and then, she had left him to Allena to care for. Hattie immediately chastised herself for such thoughts. Trouble has a way of siftin' and sortin' things out. She hoped maybe Darcy's illness had laid her down long enough to straighten out what was really important. Hattie would continue to pray that

Darcy wake up and realize what a blessed woman she was to have such a fine husband and son.

Emery bowed and turned. "This way, ma'am."

Baby Zack took his father's hand, and they followed Emery and Hattie up the wide stairway. The boy was fascinated with the steps. Rambling ranch houses seldom need stairs.

Hattie followed Emery. She glanced around at the elegance and remembered the grandeur of a couple of houses in Georgia where she had worked before she went to Texas.

"How is Miss Darcy, Emery?" Zack asked. Funny he should refer to his wife as "Miss Darcy." Probably because that is what the servants always called her.

"She had a bad night, sir, much pain." He led them down the hall, carrying luggage to the nursery, a large room containing a small bed Darcy had slept in when Baby Zack's age and a larger bed for her nanny. One wall was lined with shelves containing books, toys, and games. They looked as though they were eager and waiting for a child to come play with them.

Sarah Whitney slipped out of Darcy's rooms, closed the door quietly, and met them in the hall with a sigh of relief, hands outstretched in welcome. "You're here!" she called softly and hurried toward them. "Oh Zack! I'm so glad you are finally here. She's been calling for you."

Zack walked toward his mother-in-law and folded both her hands in his and lifted them to his lips. Her smile was gracious as usual, but Zack read her eyes, which relayed the hurt in her heart. Lines had etched her extreme tiredness in her face. "How is she?"

Sarah squeezed his hands, pursed her lips and shook her head and tightened her lips to keep from crying.

"The doctors say they have done all they can do for the moment. Her body will have to do its own healing." Tears welled and she shook her head. "Oh Zack, you'll be shocked when you see her. You won't recognize your beautiful wife." She took several deep breaths before she could continue. "It was an awful accident. All we can figure out is that the team must have spooked, bolted, and raced down the street. The buggy turned completely over, throwing her out, and the team dragged her with it. The doctor said Darcy must have landed on her back, which is broken; plus she has multiple breaks in one arm and both her legs." Sarah's tears traced a fresh wet track over her cheeks, and her lips trembled. "It's a wonder she's alive."

As they entered Darcy's suite, Darcy's soft, pitiful moaning could be heard from the bedroom. The intense agony behind the sounds clutched Zack's heart. He passed through the little sitting room, walked into the familiar bedroom and over to the motionless, moaning body of his wife. Standing here beside her in what used to be their bedroom, he still thought of her as his wife. He perched carefully on the edge of the bed, folded her limp hand into both of his, leaned over, and gently kissed her cheek. "Darcy? Darcy, it's Zack, I'm here." He lifted her limp hand to his lips and kissed it.

Slowly, Darcy opened her swollen eyes, stared at him out of two slits for a long moment with wavering, unbelieving eyes, then opened her mouth and emitted an agonized wail that seemed to come from her innermost depth. "Zaa-ack!" she cried and her eyes clung to his face.

Zack leaned over her, smitten by the fear that poured from her eyes. He had never, ever seen her so helpless, so dependent, so out of control. He couldn't suppress the thought that even during her contrived temper tantrums she had always been in control and charmingly manipulative. Zack shook his head in sympathy. To have always been in command and now stripped of everything must be sheer terror and devastating to her spirit.

Her wild, blurry eyes clung to his and locked him into her stare. He felt a slight pressure of her fingers in his hand, so he leaned over and kissed her lightly on the cheek. "Darcy—" was all his choked throat would allow.

She kept her intense, terror-filled eyes anchored on Zack's face as if she was trying to tell him something. Her lips quivered in an effort to form words but there was no sound. Her eyes grew desperate and she fitfully tossed her head back and forth then closed her eyes with a low moan.

Zack ached to help her. He would have gathered her into his arms to calm her obvious fear but was afraid to touch her for fear he would hurt her. She was almost completely wrapped in bandages. He leaned over and gently placed his cheek on hers.

She emitted a whimpering cry and Zack felt a slight twitching of her fingers. *O God, how can I help her, what can I do?*

Sarah laid her hand on Zack's shoulder, left them alone, but soon returned leading Baby Zack, followed by Hattie. She moved to the other side of the bed and lifted her grandson. "Darcy, I'm holding Baby Zack. Thank you, my daughter, for this sweet child. He's a precious boy."

Darcy's eyes shot open and locked on her mother a moment then moved to her son. Tears flowed in steady streams down the sides of her face and her lips labored over "m-my—s-son."

Sarah daubed her daughter's tears with a handkerchief then sat Baby Zack on the side of the bed beside his mother.

Darcy stared at her son who stared back at her. He reached his hand and touched her shoulder. "Mama?"

Darcy began to cry and tossed her head from side to side, growing more agitated by the minute.

Sarah picked up Baby Zack. "I'm going to take the boy downstairs. I'm sure it's too hard for him to understand why his mother can't talk to him."

"No!" Zack objected. "He needs to be here with his mother."

Quick surprise in his mother-in-law's face at the tone of his voice made him apologize.

Sara sat her grandson down gently on the bed beside Darcy and stood motionless at the side of the bed.

Zack leaned forward. "We're here, Darcy, to help you fight and get well. You are going to have to help by resting to allow your body to heal. Everything is being taken care of. You just concentrate on getting well." He leaned over and kissed her and his heart sank within him. His mind swarmed with confusion. What should he do? The divorce had been Darcy's and her father's doing. He had not been given any say in it. But she was the mother of his son! Exactly where did his loyalty lie now? He searched his legal mind but it gave him no answers.

His heart searched for words to pray. How much prayer does it take for God to hear you in your need? Zack had never given a whole lot of serious thought to prayer, although he had prayed all his remembered life as a little boy and a young man. But that had been kid stuff. He secretly admitted he hadn't needed prayer a whole lot as he grew older. In truth, he had always counted on his father and mother to do the real praying in the family.

An old memory took shape in his mind and quickly transported him to a time when as a young boy he had happened upon his father praying aloud in the barn. Zack had heard him pray in church and return thanks at mealtime, but it had been the first time he had heard his father pray alone. It was so passionate Zack had held his breath and stiffened his back against a stall wall so as not to interrupt his father with his loud thumping heart. He had felt as if he were witnessing and hearing something he shouldn't, so private it was wrong to even listen.

Still he had squatted behind the bales of hay, fascinated, scarcely breathing, fearful of being found evesdropping as he listened to his father bare his soul aloud before God. Suddenly there was silence, a long pause, then a soft "In Jesus' name, Amen." His father's boots thudded across the dirt floor and out of the barn.

The memory of that prayer stunned him more now than when he first heard it and convicted him for his lack of awareness and preparation to pray for his ailing wife. He had been brought up to believe that men should be self-sufficient and learn to handle whatever they came up against. Up to this moment, he had felt completely confident that there wasn't much he couldn't handle. He was wrong.

Darcy tossed her head fitfully back and forth. She opened her mouth as if to speak but only an agonizing sound came forth. Her eyes fluttered open and moved wildly around the room. She flung one hand in the air. Zack caught it, enclosed it in his, and rested his lips on it. She settled and a slight smile crossed her lips. "Ar—thur" she moaned then closed her eyes and settled.

Zack felt her grip release and his own heart stop. *Arthur? Who is Arthur?* The old familiar wave of helplessness engulfed him, followed by a slow kindling of anger that almost smothered him. He looked across at his son, who sat quietly on the other side of the bed, staring at his mother.

Sarah's smile faded into despair.

Suddenly, Baby Zack scooched off the side of the bed and ran to his father.

Hattie suddenly stepped to the bed, reached for Darcy's wrist and stood head down, brows knit, and fingered her pulse. She moved her fingers around the woman's wrist then looked at Zack. "You better get the doctor. Her color don't look good, and her pulse is growin' awful weak."

Sarah was out of the room before Hattie finished speaking. "Emery, send for Dr. Halston! Tell him we need him right away."

eleven

Dr. Josiah Corbett hustled up the stairs behind Emery, his medical bag gripped tightly in his hand.

Thomas and Sarah met him with concerned faces at the door of Darcy's bedroom.

"Oh, doctor, I'm so glad you're here. We've—"

"Hush, Sarah, let the doctor get to his work," Thomas said gruffly.

Sarah stepped aside.

Dr. Corbett pushed past them both to his patient's bedside. "Everyone out of the room, except Sarah," he stated flatly.

"Everyone? I'm her father, Doc," Thomas said.

The doctor raised his eyebrows, grinned, and shook his head. "Fathers and husbands are sometimes the worst. You can come back in after I've examined her." He herded the men to the door, and they dutifully filed into the hall. Dr. Corbett closed the door behind them.

Zack stood with his back to the wall, an uncomfortable place where he seemed to find himself too often lately. He couldn't fight it. Darcy was the mother of his son. Seeing her again, so helpless, his mind kept searching for a way to draw upon that first happy year of their life together. They had been head over heels in love with each other. Or so he had thought. He had even learned to enjoy some of the parties as he became better acquainted with the Boston social set. It was made up mostly of professional men and their wives who were advantageous for Zack and Darcy to know.

Then Thomas gradually enlarged Zack's work load until even Darcy complained. On some evenings when he had come home early, she had already gone to dinner with her friends, so Zack ate his late dinner alone in the dining room served by the maid, Sylvia.

Then young men began coming to escort her. Zack remembered how jealous he had felt toward these stylish young men who were so attentative to his new wife. But Darcy had laughed and calmed his fears by telling him that to be seen with Darcy and Thomas Whitney was advantageous for young men trying to become prominent lawyers in Boston and that it also helped them mingle in the right circles of society.

It was true. At one time he had been one of them. Also, Darcy had reminded him it was not proper in Boston for a lady to go places without an escort and that these nice young men were just friends helping her attend the parties when he couldn't go. Secretly, he had been glad. The parties had grown to be a bore going to the same places, doing the same things with the same people. Zack remembered how disillusioned he became when he finally admitted to himself that if Darcy and Thomas had their way he would always be just one of the associate firm lawyers and able to go only so far under Thomas.

Back home in Texas, his dream and goal had been to become a lawyer, have his own law firm, and help bring law and order to Texas. There was a growing need for interpretation of the law, since Texas had finally seceded from Mexico, joined the union, and become a state. He had even dreamed of becoming a Texas state legislator. Texas needed him. A slow grin spread across Zack's face and he admitted "And I need Texas." It was man's country. "Once a Texas boy, always a Texas boy." Yep. His mother had been right.

Zack remembered he'd had to use all his accumulated courtroom powers of persuasion to get Darcy to agree to leave Boston. He knew she wasn't happy in Texas when she changed into a petulant, childish woman and the bane of his family. He appreciated their patience as they all tried to help her adjust. Zack knew she missed the concerts, parties, and picnics yet had hoped she'd settle and adjust as she got acquainted with the ranchers and their wives and got involved in the general work. He now regretted it had taken him so long to realize that she had no intention of doing any such thing. "I hate ranch life," she spit out finally during one of their almost daily arguments. "It's dirty, smelly, and unrefined, and I hate it here."

After that Darcy had refused to attend any of the rancher's socials and too often rode out alone even when Zack asked her not to. There were wild animals and sometimes unfriendly Indians, treacherous terrain. . . It bore no resemblence to the Boston Commons.

He remembered the first time Darcy stated she was just homesick and insisted she just had to go home for a while. Naively, he thought it might help her wean herself from Boston. But when he had helped her board the train she had looked into his eyes and flatly stated, "I'm not coming back, Zack. If you want me for your wife, it has to be in Boston." At the time, he ignored her comment. It had come from her homesickness. They loved each other. They had a son. She needed him. He needed her. She was his wife.

He should have known but didn't want to accept the fact that she meant it. Now only an agreement upon property settlement lay between Zack and the finality of the divorce. He had refused to sign any final papers till he discussed a number of things with Thomas. Zack hated an inner gut feeling he couldn't shake off—a gnawing suspicion that his father-in-law would wipe him clean if he could. Knowing Thomas, he had thoroughly investigated his family's holdings in Texas and—

The bedroom door opened.

Dr. Corbett walked to the two men. "I've adjusted the brace on her back and her leg to keep it as immobile as possible till she heals. She is in a lot of pain, but I've given her a pain potion, and I'll leave some with Sarah."

"Will she be able to walk again?" Thomas asked abruptly.

"That I don't know. It depends on the way her back and leg bones heal and work—many things. I don't know how much damage has been done to the nerves. I'm sorry she lost the baby. That weakened her body even more."

Zack's mouth dropped open. He stared at Dr. Corbett. "Lost the—baby? What baby?"

From the look on his father-in-law's face, it was as big a surprise to Thomas as it was to Zack.

"The fetus was only about two, maybe three months old. It was a surprise to me, too, gentlemen. Darcy hadn't mentioned anything about it but she must have known."

Two or three months! Zack's stomach churned. Darcy had been in Boston four months.

His father-in-law shot a quick glance at Zack, his face a storm cloud. He turned back to the doctor. "Did Sarah know?"

"I don't think so. If she had I'm sure that would have been one of the first questions Sarah would have asked right after the accident, out of concern for both Darcy and the baby." Dr. Corbett turned to Zack and patted his shoulder. "I'm sorry, son."

Zack nodded stiffly and tried to swallow the awkward

lump in his throat. His body was suddenly awash with weariness, and he felt like an out-and-out coward for wishing he, Baby Zack, and Hattie were on a train going west. When one isn't loved or wanted—

Suddenly, Thomas turned on his heel and left the room without a word.

Dr. Corbett slowly put his coat on and closed his bag. He patted Zack on the shoulder again. "I'm sorry I can't give you more hope, but many of her injuries are internal and as yet have given us no signs they are serious."

Zack reached for Dr. Corbett's hand and shook it. "I know you are doing everything possible to help her."

The doctor nodded and smiled. "Thank you. Let me know if she becomes restless. I've left more powder packets on the table if you need them. I'll be back tomorrow." He picked up his bag and left.

Zack's chest ached. He walked over, sat down on the chair beside Darcy's bed, reached for her limp, cool hand, and held it in his. He took a deep breath and exhaled it slowly through his lips to relieve the heaviness he felt inside.

Darcy lay quiet.

Dr. Corbett said the powdered potion he had just given her must be taking effect so it should make her sleep.

Zack watched her breast laboriously rise and fall. It seemed to grow more shallow with each labored breath. Every so often, she moved her head slightly and moaned.

A disturbing thought surfaced in Zack's mind. *Had Darcy ever at any time in her life accepted the Lord Jesus as her Savior? Sometime in her childhood, perhaps?* He'd have to ask Sarah. He knew Sarah was a strong believer who from the beginning of her marriage had courageously faced her petulant husband every Sunday noon at dinner because she had insisted on taking Darcy to Sunday school and church, which made Sunday dinner one-half hour later than Thomas liked.

Zack admired that little woman's spunk.

He remembered right after he and Darcy were married they had joined Sarah and gone to church with her. Then there were Sundays when Darcy complained "she didn't feel well" or some other excuse she could find not to go. Finally she plain refused to get up and go.

The subterfuge would finally end when he and Sarah went to church while Darcy rested in bed without excuse after a Saturday evening festivity. Thomas, as usual, spent Sunday morning riding his horse on the park trail.

One particular Sunday morning rose in his mind. He and Sarah had arrived home from church a few minutes later than usual. Thomas had grumbled all through dinner about their being late and had vehemently expressed his summation of religion in one word. *Foolishness!*

Another Sunday he became more vocal and said he thought that all people who attended church were wasting their time. He had guffawed at how easily they allowed themselves to be bilked out of their hard-earned money. "Anyone who believes in a man who lived centuries ago, supposedly was raised from the dead, and called himself the Son of God is an addlebrained weakling—a crybaby who never has enough gumption to learn to stand on his or her own two feet."

Zack sighed. Unfortunately, early in his marriage, he had reluctantly discovered his beautiful wife believed as her father. Now, to his chagrin, in his strong desire to become a distinguished Boston lawyer, Zack admitted, he had compromised and pushed aside his own deeper, personal beliefs and feelings to accommodate his wife and father-in-law. He could do it no more. He decided to establish his own law firm in Texas. When Darcy was well, they would buy a house in the state capital and live there.

Suddenly, a memory of his own father surfaced in Zack's mind. He had been fifteen. They were out riding the range during roundup which was when they did a lot of man-talk.

"When you choose a wife, son," his father had advised, "be sure she is a Christian woman who knows the Lord Jesus as her Savior. The Bible strongly advises both men and women not to become unequally yoked with unbelievers." Zack now wished he had followed his father's advice.

Darcy moaned, opened her eyes and stared at him.

He leaned over and kissed her.

Her eyes pleaded with him, then closed, and she seemed to settle.

Early the next morning Zack was summoned by his father-in-law to his law office, hopefully, he said, to get a few things settled. He watched Thomas's well-planned movements. He could read him like a book. This sudden meeting was to hurriedly get holdings settled if—or before Darcy died. If she died, Thomas would be stripped of any legal power in Zack's life. His inheritance in the Circle Z and the custody of his son would belong to him alone. Zack's chest ached. He felt like a sitting duck perched temporarily on an uncomfortable hard rock, waiting for some little bad boy to throw a rock at him.

twelve

The next afternoon Zack sat by Darcy's bed again. She had not responded since the doctor left. He watched her labored breathing grow more shallow with every breath. Her eyelids fluttered open and her glassy eyes stared at Zack for a moment then shut again and she quieted.

Zack inhaled a long, deep sigh and his spirit thought of Darcy's salvation. Had he failed as the spiritual leader of his family that his father had told him every man should be? What's a man to do when his wife refuses or ignores his guidance? Force is not the way. In his practice of law he had seen too much of that and the devastation it heaped on families.

He looked down at the little boy sitting on the chair beside him, who had been very quiet. He stretched forth his arms.

Baby Zack hopped down from the chair, climbed onto his father's lap, and nestled into the crook of his arm. His wide questioning eyes stared up into Zack's face. "Mama sick?"

Zack nodded. "Yes and we are going to pray she'll get well, aren't we?"

As if on cue, Baby Zack bowed his head.

Zack recognized his mother's training and smiled. He picked up Darcy's limp hand lying on top of the quilt and his son's small hand, folded the three together and bowed his head. "Father in heaven, here we are, three of your children who need your help. My son and I ask that you heal his mother and make her well again—" Zack paused and swallowed. "We pray in the name of Jesus, your Son and our Savior." He opened his eyes and found his son's gaze pinned to his face.

"Where is Jesus?"

Zack smiled. "He's everywhere, in heaven, or wherever people need him to be." Zack smoothed away the frown between the pinched brows of his son's forehead. How do you explain to a child what you do not fully understand yourself?

The child's eyes spoke questions he wasn't old enough to form into words. "Why doesn't Jesus just come here and make Mama better?"

The innocence of a child. Zack smiled. "Jesus is always here. Don't you remember the story we read in the Bible about Jesus feeding all those people on the mountain when they were hungry and about Him healing the little crippled boy? Sometimes we have to go where Jesus is."

Darcy moaned. Her breathing labored, and she tossed her head fitfully from side to side.

Baby Zack stared at his mother and snuggled closer to his father.

Zack searched for words that might enable him to explain some of this to his bewildered little son. He found none so bowed his head and spoke from his heart. "O Lord Jesus, comfort my little son. Help me to help him understand the hard, confusing things he is facing today. He's so young and I confess, Lord, I don't have all the answers."

Baby Zack stared at his father.

Zack longed for Darcy to get well if only to be given time to learn to enjoy the son she had not yet found. Her son needed her.

The door opened. Dr. Corbett and Sarah walked through.

Zack rose, nodded and took his son out into the hall while the doctor examined his patient.

As they stood together, the boy looked up. His eyes begged for answers.

Zack stooped and picked him up in his arms.

Eyes sparkling with tears, Baby Zack leaned his face on his father's shoulder. "When we go home is Mama coming home, too?"

Zack shook his head. "I hope so. We'll have to wait until the doctor tells us she is well enough to travel that far."

Dr. Corbett came out of the room. "I'd like to speak to you alone, Zack."

Sarah put her arm around Baby Zack. "Come, dear, let's go down to the kitchen. Cook made fresh cookies this morning. They should be cool enough to eat by now." Baby Zack looked back at his father, grinned, and allowed himself to be led off by his grandmother and the promise of goodies.

Dr. Corbett went back into the room, gathered his instruments into his bag and came and joined Zack. They stood in the hall.

"I'm glad I have a chance to talk to you alone, Zack, to tell you how serious Darcy's injuries are. I have done all I can do here. She has internal injuries we can only guess at, and it's getting to where I must keep her heavily sedated with powders and potions. She couldn't stand the pain otherwise. But that's not solving the problem. She was badly mangled when the carriage flipped and dragged her with it during the accident." The doctor took hold of Zack's arm and faced him. "The hospital has just received a newly invented machine called an X-ray machine. It takes pictures of what a person looks like on the inside. If we could get those pictures of Darcy, we would be able to see where she is broken. What she has really needed all along is to be in a hospital where she can be watched constantly by trained doctors and nurses but—" Dr. Corbett pursed his lips and shook his head. "But Thomas won't have it. I don't understand that man. I don't know where he gets his information but his excuse is that too many people die when they go to the hospital and that is why he hired me and private nurses to attend her here at home." He looked Zack straight in the eye. "But that's not enough! She's *not* getting the care she needs. I don't understand him. For such an intelligent man. . ." Dr. Corbett shook his head, "He seems afraid to let her out of his control. Can't he see she needs close watching and the care of a trained private nurse with a hospital doctor on constant call." The doctor looked directly into Zack's eyes. "As her husband, you could make the decision to send her to the hospital. If it is not already too late, it could save her life."

Zack felt the heavy weight of responsibility slowly settle on his shoulders. He was hung again. He was divorced but he wasn't. Thomas was using his typical tactic of controlling just enough strings to keep everyone off balance and him in charge. What self-serving reason did Thomas have in withholding the finalizing of the divorce papers? Zack had a sneaking suspicion that his father-in-law had been investigating the Circle Z holdings, gearing for a property fight. Zack faced Dr. Corbett and grinned. This time, his little game was going to kick back.

"Thomas hasn't yet given me the final dissolution papers to our divorce, so I feel I can still legally make this decision. If it will help Darcy, I say yes—you have my permission to move her to the hospital for the care she so desperately needs."

Dr. Corbett shook his hand. "Thank you, son, I'll make arrangements immediately and send the hospital ambulance wagon here as quickly as possible." He picked up his medicine bag, checked his patient, who at the moment was resting quietly, and left the room.

A little face peeked around the door frame.

"Come in, son."

Baby Zack hustled in, a cookie in each hand, climbed up on a chair beside his father, and nibbled on one. He offered his father a bite.

"Thank you, son," Zack said and broke a small piece off the cookie and popped it in his mouth. "Mmmmm. Cook makes good cookies, doesn't she?"

Baby Zack nodded then bit off another piece.

A sudden commotion rose from the lower hall. Raised voices and a slamming door brought Zack to attention. He wasn't surprised the noise was followed by angry footsteps on the stairs and a determined walk down the hall. It was Thomas. Zack took a deep breath and prepared to defend himself.

Thomas stormed in like a thunderous cloud. "How dare you make a decision about my daughter with the doctor without consulting me. I am her father!"

Zack grinned. It looked as if Thomas's carefully laid plan had fallen apart. "But because you have dragged your feet on the divorce, I am still legally her husband therefore I have the final say. I checked out the papers at the office the other day, Thomas. You are withholding the final papers for some reason you haven't told me yet."

Thomas snorted and ignored him. "You have no right to make such a decision. I told the doctor I will not allow my daughter to be experimented on by some new fly-by-night crazy medical machine."

Zack faced him. "Thomas, if there is something that will help Darcy get well, and Dr. Corbett approves, then I think we should take his advice. He knows a lot more about making people well than you or I do."

Thomas stared a hole through him. "You have no right—"

Zack almost felt guilty at the smug feel of victory that surged through him. "Yes I have. You gave me that right by withholding the final divorce papers from being finalized in court. The divorce papers I saw at the office were not legally finalized. Darcy is still my legal wife. Therefore as her husband, I have the final say." Zack couldn't suppress his grin. His father-in-law's craftily made plans had backfired.

Thomas's snapping eyes flung daggers. He swung on his heel and stomped out of the room.

Zack inhaled a deep breath and exhaled it slowly to quell the tightness of his chest.

Darcy moaned, suddenly became agitated, and began tossing her head fitfully back and forth.

Zack hurried to her bedside. Could it have been possible she heard them?

She whimpered. Her mouth tried to form words that came out like moans and grunting noises and made no sense. Had she been conscious enough to hear what he and her father had said? Poor girl. She didn't need any more problems.

Baby Zack, face upturned, stared at his father, his little brows pinched together. His lips quivered.

The bewildered look on his little son's face tugged Zack's heart. How frightening and bewildering it must be for a child to see adults argue, particularly members of their own family. Zack had never heard either his

mother nor his father argue or even say an unkind word
to each other in all his life. He shot a grateful prayer of
thanks heavenward for the caring, Christian parents he
had been given. The more he lived as a grown man, the
more he found something to thank them for every day.
Until now, he hadn't realized how blessed he had been to
have a God-fearing father and mother who had respected
and lived the truth.

Sarah hurried into the room to Darcy's bedside, picked
up her daughter's hand, and perched nervously on the
side of the bed. Her swollen, teary eyes betrayed her.

Poor Sarah. Zack's heart ached for this good woman.
Thomas had vented his anger on her, as usual. Zack had
heard his blustering and shouting below. She always
seemed to get the blunt end of everything in this family.
Sarah glanced nervously toward the door as the thundering boots of her husband pounded up the stairs. She
leaned over, kissed her daughter on the cheek, and
smoothed her hair.

Zack walked over and patted her shoulder. "Don't be
worried, Sarah. Hospitals are not allowed to use new
machines unless they are thoroughly tested and approved.
Who knows, this may be a healing machine of the
future."

Sarah shook her head and said softly. "I don't know
about the machines. I want her to go so she'll get better
care than we can give her here." She reached into her
dress pocket for her handkerchief, daubed her eyes, and
wiped her nose.

"Mother," Zack hadn't called her that in a long time.

"The hospitals test and test these new machines
before they use them on patients." He took her two
shaking hands in his and looked intently into her eyes.
"Sarah, now is when we test our faith." He looked down

into Sarah's pain-filled eyes. "God has a lot of wayward children and still loves them same as he does us. I think he encourages us to try and help them any and every way available to us."

Sarah looked up, her lips quivering, her eyes swimming with tears.

Zack's heart went out to her. A small woman in stature but tall and brave in spirit. He had always admired her courage and the inner strength he knew it must take to live with such a dominating husband.

On impulse, Zack suddenly gathered her into his arms and held her. "You can cry, Sarah, your husband isn't here."

At first, she fought. Finally the dam broke.

Zack held her for a few moments; then she sank into the rocker beside the bed, bent over, buried her face in her hands and sobbed.

"Mo-ther."

Sarah gasp, bolted upright, and rushed to Darcy's side.

Darcy peeked through tiny open slits in each eye.

"I'm here, child." Tears streamed down Sarah's face.

"Yesss—" Darcy's voice was a gasping whisper.

Sarah sat on the side of the bed, leaned over, and gently gathered her child in her arms as best she could without hurting her. "I'm here, dear. I won't leave you."

Darcy strained to pull her eyelids half open then fixed her gaze on her mother. "Moth-er." The sick girl tried to stretch her lips into a smile but only managed to settle a peaceful look on her face. Suddenly, her eyes sprung wide open. She made a feeble effort to rise, gasped, released one long shivering breath, and relaxed into her mother's arms.

Zack rushed to Darcy, grabbed her wrist, and searched

for a pulse. He couldn't find it. There was none.

Sarah's face pleaded with Zack. Blinding tears ran down her cheeks. Sarah pulled Darcy into her arms, rocked back and forth, and quietly cried.

Zack leaned over and put his arms around them both. Baby Zack ran to them and stretched forth his little arms. Zack and Sarah gathered him in.

A gruff voice and heavy boots invaded the downstairs hall, stomped up the stairs, and resounded along the hall-way. Thomas thundered into the room and boomed, "Darcy is not leaving here. I told the hospital I forbid them to use her to test their new machine—" He stopped abruptly.

Everyone was huddled over Darcy on the bed.

Thomas moved to the bed. "What's going on here?"

Sarah's soft, muffled sobs escaped into the room.

Zack stood and the two men's eyes met. "It's over. Darcy's dead," Zack said in a husky voice. "You lost the case."

thirteen

"Harness, Texas!" the conductor called as he entered the coach car and walked through. "Harness, Texas!"

Zack rose and pulled the luggage from the hat rack and under the seat.

Baby Zack watched wide-eyed then tried to wiggle free from Hattie's strong hold.

"Sit still, child, your father will get you in a minute." She tightened her hold and turned to the window. The station came into view. Hattie pointed. "Look! There's your grandma and uncle Tom and aunt Mary Lou and the twins. They're here to meet us. They must have received the wireless we sent."

Baby Zack pressed his face against the glass, giggled, and waved and waved until the train slowly jerked to a stop. The twins had run alongside the train, jumping, waving, and calling to him. He squirmed and tried to slide off Hattie's lap.

"Sit still, son, till the train stops." Zack piled a barricade of luggage on the aisle seat.

The family waiting outside scanned the passengers one by one as they came down the steps. Finally Zack's tall form filled the opening. He stepped down, lifted his eager son and luggage to the ground, and helped Hattie manage the last big step.

Baby Zack immediately raced to Tommy. They stood and grinned at each other. Beth skipped over to them and threw her arms around Baby Zack. He shook her off. The two boys ignored her.

Two Circle Z ranch wagons waited. Allena grabbed Baby Zack, boarded one, sat him on her lap, and planted a kiss on his cheek. He frowned and wiped it off. She grinned and nodded knowingly. He was growing up. She glanced at Zack. "We're all very sorry about Darcy, but thank God her suffering is over. As I understand she was seriously injured, wasn't she?"

Zack nodded his head.

"Now the Lord has other plans for you, son, so we bow to them."

Zack smiled. Those words had a familiar ring. It surprised him that he remembered them. His mother had made that same statement when they had returned from his father's funeral. He had been twelve. They had sounded cruel to him then—like a slap in his father's face. The aching hollow spot in his young heart had resented the way the family brushed its hands and seemed to get on with business as usual. His father's absence had been unbearable for him that first year. Zack had felt, since he was the oldest son, he must assume his father's responsibility to his mother and take the place of his father. He now knew that if it hadn't been for that concern to take his father's place his world without his father would have left an unbearable hole. What he understood now he wouldn't have been able to accept at twelve. Death has such a final ring to it. You can't change it. You can't escape it. It's a callous, hard, cold fact of life everyone has to face some time or other. His lawyer mind now analyzed his feelings. *At first, one is bereft, steps aside from life and wraps his arms round the hurt and loss to ease the pain. But the time comes when one has to settle his feelings about it, no matter what those feelings are and move with it.* He remembered it had taken him a long time to feel life had any semblance of normal after his father died. His absence had created a desperate lonely ache in his chest that took a long time to go away, and even yet, as old as he was, he still missed his father.

With Darcy, it was different, somehow. Zack was almost ashamed to admit that the heavy stone he had been carrying in his heart and spirit during the years of their married life had eased. Reflecting back, he had hung in limbo most of the time, never knowing what to expect. He was ashamed to admit the only emotion he felt now was a settling relief. It was over. He could get on with his life. *God forgive me for such selfish feelings.* He took a deep breath. As it released, the burden of unfinished business seemed to ease off his chest.

"—so Tex and Lily are pretty well settled in their new home. Lots of finishing to do, but it's livable."

Zack was suddenly aware his mother had been talking and he hadn't heard a word she had said. He stabbed at an answer. "Good," he said.

The twins giggled and wiggled among the luggage in the back of Tom's wagon ahead of him.

Zack smiled. Watching their bobbing heads and hearing their carefree laughter carried him back to his childhood and the carefree joy he had known then. He almost envied them their carefree life. But a man with family has responsibilities and accepts them. Their day would come. Zack inhaled deeply. His spirit relaxed and settled. He wouldn't want life any other way. Thank God for responsibilities and the joy that hides in the midst of them.

When the wagons rolled under the familiar Circle Z arch, Zack took a deep breath and exhaled slowly. It was time to begin again.

The conversation at the dinner table was mostly from

Zack and Hattie as they told of the events of the past weeks. At first, Zack shied and would rather have avoided the subject, but as he and Hattie told it from their different views he felt the settling of a warm sense of peace.

"My heart goes out to Sarah," Hattie commented. "What a strong spirit she has to have to live each day. I admire her."

So did Zack. A new thought took root. He turned to Nelson. "Nelson, would you be able to paint a picture of Baby Zack to send to his grandmother, Sarah?"

Nelson grinned. "I don't see why not. I'll need help from someone to keep him still and occupied long enough to pose for a basic outline, and I think I can handle it after that."

Hattie spoke up. "Oh, Sarah would love that. I felt so sorry to part her from her grandson when she handed Baby Zack to me when we left. She adores him. From what I learned about her on our visit she's my kind of strong, unsinkable lady."

Zack nodded. "That she is and a brave one." No words were said about his father-in-law and no one asked. It was just as well. Least said is still the easiest mended. How many times had his mother said that. Again he found his mother had known what she was talking about.

As the daylight waned, Tom and Mary Lou gathered their twins to head for home. As usual, the children begged to play some more. "Tomorrow," Tom said, swooped his son into his arms, sat him up on his shoulders, and Mary Lou and Beth followed him. They waved and turned to the path that led to their house. It was painted with dancing, silvery moonbeams.

"I can't help but feel sad and glad at the same time," Mary Lou said as they walked along. "Perhaps now

Zack's life can begin to take shape so he can concentrate and get on with building his law practice."

Tom nodded. Yes, a whole new life stood ready and waiting to open up for his brother. He would be free to seize the opportunities that were now open to him to become a representative or senator for the state of Texas. *He'd be a good one,* Tom mused.

Mary Lou helped her children into their nightclothes, listened to their prayers, kissed them, tucked them into bed, said good night, and walked to the kitchen door. She could see a lantern light bouncing across doors and windows inside the barn as Tom made rounds of his night chores at the barn. She pushed her new screen door open and slid onto her restin' chair just outside her kitchen door, laid her head back against the outside wall, and lifted her face to the gentle, warm, evening breeze that brushed her warm cheeks.

She placed her hand on her stomach. She would tell Tom her special secret tonight. She had wanted to be sure. Three months. The timing was good. The twins were four.

Her thoughts soared to Kansas and Pa and Aunt Nelda. In Nelda's last letter Mary Lou almost read between the lines that there might be a chance of her and Pa coming to visit now that the railroads were fanning everywhere across the country and had connected Kansas with Texas.

Mary Lou smiled and hoped they would come. She and Tom had even talked about them getting older, and perhaps the time would come when they would live with them. Pa would like their ranch. That had been his dream at one time before his accident. Dare she ever hope that Pa might consent to their moving to Texas and living with her and Tom? She wanted her father to watch his grandchildren grow. She knew they would be delighted with all the time he could probably spend with them. Mary Lou sighed and raised her eyes to heaven. "Mama, you always said, 'When you dream and pray, do it big, 'cause we have a great, loving Father in heaven who delights in giving good gifts to his children'." Mary Lou lowered her eyes, smiled, then looked up again. "Lord, I'm prayin' big tonight!"

Her heart soared. She blushed at her untoward audacity toward her heavenly Father.

"Your heavenly Father has cattle on a thousand hills, plenty for all his children'." Mama used to say. "All you have to do is ask Him!"

Mary Lou remembered she and Mama had done a lot of "askin'." For Pa's safety when he traveled. For rain and sunshine. For the vegetable garden to grow a good crop. Even for the little hurt rabbit Mary Lou had found in the field one day and brought home.

Pa had wanted to shoot it to "put it out of its misery," he said and have Mama make rabbit stew.

The very thought of the poor, helpless little thing being shot broke Mary Lou's heart, and she had cried and wailed and pleaded for Pa to let her keep it. Finally, Mama had told Pa that she and Mary Lou would nurse it back to health and care for it, then let it go.

Pa had harrumphed and said, "Don't come to me when it gets into your vegetable garden." But he let Mary Lou keep it.

The rabbit had been Mary Lou's first pet till it was full grown, and then one day, it disappeared.

Mama had held her in her arms to comfort her while she cried. "My child, it is the same with all things. Everything must move on. Things never stay the same. When it's time, it's time. That's how we learn." Mama had cupped Mary Lou's teary face in her hand and smiled. "And someday that rabbit will be a papa and have a family. I'll bet he'll be a proud papa."

That had been a new thought for Mary Lou. She smiled now as she remembered that whenever she saw a rabbit in her yard, she wondered if it was part of "her" papa rabbit's family.

Mary Lou raised her face to the heavens and closed her eyes. "Thank you, Mama, for all my good memories." Her chest ached. If Mama could only see her grand-children.

And who says she doesn't?

Mary Lou's heart almost burst with joy. Her heartache released and flew upward and she lifted her face to the sky. "I bet you watch us every day, don't you, Mama?" Mary Lou knew it had to be, sometimes Mama seemed so close. . .

The quiet night whispered its answer with a soft, gentle breeze that blew Mary Lou's hair. No. There were no voices. Just a shower of comforting assurance that bloomed comforting thoughts and snuggled them into her heart.

Warm tears slid down Mary Lou's cheeks and freshened the wings of her thank-you prayer as it ascended to her heavenly Father. She closed her eyes and relaxed.

Tom finished the last of the chores, stuck the pitchfork upright in the hay, and closed the doors of the barn to keep out the wolves. The evening air cooled the perspiration on his brow and his damp shirt. He turned toward the house.

He spotted Mary Lou on her restin' chair and grinned. "Trying to get a breath of fresh air" was the excuse she always gave. As he neared, he slowed down and walked quietly and grinned. She was asleep. He wasn't surprised.

It was only when the twins were asleep in bed she could relax. He walked softly and stood looking down into her face. It hadn't changed since the day he married her, only more mature, more lovely.

She was beautiful. His heart swelled within him. He tipped his head from side to side and grinned. Hmmm. She was gaining a bit of matronly weight through her middle. He pursed his lips. He'd better not voice that observation.

Mary Lou slowly opened her eyes; then they popped wide open when she saw Tom standing before her. "Oh! I didn't even hear you come up!"

Tom smiled at her.

"How long have you been here?"

"Just a minute or so. You were sleepin' so peaceful I didn't want to disturb my beautiful wife and took the rare opportunity to just stand and look at her." Tom grinned. "I have to admit I had an awful hard time not bending over and kissing you."

Mary Lou laughed and stood up. "If you open your arms I'll find my way into them."

As his arms folded around her Mary Lou felt a joyous sense of peace and safety. Tom's strong arms were her haven of rest, her place to release her cares and bask in the love she felt there.

He gave her a long, lingering kiss.

It was the right time. Nestled in his arms she smiled and looked into his blue, blue eyes. "I have some news to tell you."

"Oh?" Tom's eyebrows pinched in question.

"We have a new baby coming to increase our family."

Tom's brows raised and a big smile spread across his face.

Mary Lou nodded. "In about six months or so, we

can expect a little bundle from heaven."

Tom threw his head back, laughed, lifted her into his arms, and spun her around before he set her back on her feet. "Best news I've had in a long time. Much better than a new calf or colt!"

"Tom!"

"Just kidding. I'm proud. We could have a dozen and I wouldn't—"

Mary Lou threw horrified hands into the air. "Oh, please. Let's not overdo it."

Tom cupped her face. The love in his eyes melted her heart. "I love you, Mary Lou," he said huskily. "You have far exceeded my highest expectations of how wonderful a wife could be."

Mary Lou nodded. "I feel the same love for you, Tom."

His arms tenderly gathered her to him, and he held her tenderly pressed against him—the safest place in her whole world. Her spirit rose in thanksgiving to her heavenly Father for this dear, sweet man He had given her for a husband. *My cup runneth over* flooded her mind.

Tom kissed her softly, released her, opened the door, and they went inside.

Zillions of stars in a wide, blue-black sky twinkled "Good night!"

fourteen

"Hello! Hello!"

Familiar voices.

Mary Lou hurried from her bedroom to the kitchen door to greet Allena and Laura. They released Baby Zack, whose sturdy, little legs flew him to the barn calling "Tommy, I comin'!"

Laura entered the kitchen puffing. "I do believe that road gets steeper and longer every time I travel it." She cupped her hands under her stomach to help ease the weight and sought a chair.

Mary Lou laughed. "It isn't the road that's longer or the grade that's steeper, it's the burden that gets heavier." It wouldn't be long till she would carry a similar load. But for now, it would be Tom's and her secret. She knew she wouldn't be able to hide it for long. Hattie had gazed at her with observant eyes the other day when she was down at the main ranch. That wise, little bird may have surmised the truth but always minded her own business. Bless her. Their secret was safe.

Mary Lou turned to her stove. The boiling teakettle rattled and steamed its readiness. She spooned tea leaves into Mama's big, old teapot Aunt Nelda had insisted she take home with her when they visited last year. It had been Mama's favorite.

Laura placed cups and saucers on the table then plopped herself on a chair and took several deep breaths. "Mary Lou, how on earth did you ever carry two?"

"The same way you are carrying one except it was

a double load."

The women laughed and withdrew into their own thoughts, remembering.

Mary Lou set a pan of cinnamon biscuits she had made that morning and a small jar of her precious berry jam on the table. The tea kettle whistled, she made tea, snuggled Mama's tea cozy over the pot, and sat down.

"Has anyone seen Lily since the wedding?" Mary Lou asked. "Tom told Tex to take a week off for their honeymoon, but they came home after four days. Tom said Tex appeared at our barn right after they got home 'cause he was concerned about the new colt's knee. Then finally he admitted he and Lily got homesick and were eager to get back to their new home and children."

The women laughed.

"Oh these men pretend to be such tough birds but most are really like old mother hens when it comes to their families and animals," Allena commented. "I remember one day I told my Zachary I thought he loved his horses more than he loved me." Allena grinned at the raised eyebrows and surprised expressions of the younger women.

"What did he say?" Mary Lou asked.

"Being the gallant gentleman he was he said his horses only gave him obedience, loyalty, and money, but I gave him the most important things, love, a wife, and family."

The women nodded and withdrew into their own thoughts.

"Well I don't even keep count anymore of the number of nights Tom spends in the barn, especially when our mares are ready to foal or a horse is sick," Mary Lou admitted. "But he has saved many a colt or filly who might not have made it if he hadn't been there.

Tom says he has a big investment in every animal we have."

"He's right. Every birth is special," Allena said quietly. "Birthing is a gift of God," Allena said quietly, "be it animal or human. It's what happens after birth that is important. It has always amazed me how much God allows us to assist Him in His work. I remember a few weak colts who lived only because Zachary rescued them from being trampled in the stall by their own mothers."

Mary Lou caught that wistful, far-off look that usually filled Allena's eyes when she talked about her late husband.

She continued, "Zachary was as concerned about his animals at birth as he was when each one of his sons was born." Allena slowly exhaled a deep breath and smiled at the women around her. "Every so often these men forget they have to be tough and show how tender-hearted they really are."

The young women smiled and nurtured their own personal memories.

"But as you each well know life can be both hard and wonderful at the same time," Allena added softly.

Was Allena allowing them to peek into a deep loneliness Mary Lou had sensed in Allena? If something ever happened to Tom—she shuddered to even think of it. Mary Lou couldn't imagine her life without him. They were as one and incomplete without the other. Mary Lou restrained herself from getting up, walking over, and putting her arms around her mother-in-law. It would have embarrassed her so she smiled and prayed instead. *Father, gather Allena into the comfort of your love and give her the peace and contentment she seems to need right now. You are now not only her God and*

Father but husband as well.

Allena glanced across the table at Mary Lou and smiled.

Mary Lou realized Allena had been staring at her. Was it possible to transfer thoughts? Yet, how else could Mary Lou sense she was thinking of her? Mary Lou was constantly amazed at how much more there was to God's spiritual world and life than she ever realized or understood. She had learned that God expresses His love in and through people and events that happen, even though many times we are not aware or realize it. *He loved us while we were yet sinners.* Mary Lou sensed she would never fully understand God's love but thanked Jesus for showing His children the great extent of Our Father's love when He died for us on the cross.

The women quietly sipped their tea.

"I talked to Ruthella at church, Sunday," Allena commented.

"She said even though it is early she and Anna are already preparing their work plans for the new school year. How fortunate we are that Ruthella is so gracious and includes Anna. Ruthella commented that getting old hadn't erased Anna's knowledge or wisdom nor her teaching ability and that there was still a lot of good teaching left in that spunky woman." Allena paused and laughed. "I remember one time Anna talked to me of a concern she had of what would happen to her when she was too old to teach, since she had no family to go to. I told her that she was a part of God's family and He would not forget her." Allena paused, sipped her tea, and added, "I remember a while back wondering what was going to happen to me when I got old. Now I know. Whether you're in the human or heavenly family, you have a place in the pasture."

The room was stilled and the women sipped their tea in quiet.

"You have a big pasture, Mother," Mary Lou finally said.

Allena looked into Mary Lou's eyes and nodded. "The *Lord* has a big pasture." She looked around the table and nodded. "I thank God for each one of you every day here in my pasture."

The women sipped their tea.

"Ruthella told me she is planning to have Anna concentrate on reading and numbers in groups, which will enable her to sit while she listens to the children read and drill them on their numbers. And Anna will grade papers, which will free Ruthella to do more individual teaching with each child on the different grade levels. They will not only accomplish twice as much, but each child will have more individual teacher attention. Our children are blessed, and I hope the parents recognize they are getting a real bargain. Two teachers for the price of one!"

"Perhaps we could gather a little extra donation from the parents sometime," Laura suggested.

"Absolutely not!" Allena stated. "If either one of them thought we were taking up a collection, they would consider it charity and their dignity would be insulted. I think the best way to help is to see to the schoolhouse and their cabin, supply them with the food they need from our ranch gardens as we always have done, and include them in with our families on holidays or family gatherings. I'm sure that will mean more than a little extra money which most of the parents cannot afford."

"Could we figure out a way to just raise Ruthella's salary?" Laura asked.

Allena shook her head. "That wouldn't work. Those

two women are too smart to fall for that. A raise later or next year, yes, but not now." She laughed. "Anyway, you don't raise a teacher's salary before she starts her job. Ruthella would catch on to that right away. Anna told me the other day she is so grateful the ranchers and Ruthella are allowing her to stay. To have a home and do what she loves to do is pay enough, she said."

Mary Lou removed the tea cozy and refilled the teacups.

The women sugared their tea, leaned back in their chairs, and sipped, relishing these rare moments of peace and a quiet time together.

Sudden squeals pierced the stillness. The children emerged from the barn and ran toward the house.

Allena and Laura rose together. "I guess it's time we're getting back."

Allena asked, "Is it alright if Tommy and Beth come home with us to play with Baby Za—" She smiled. "By the way, I must inform everyone that Zack says it's time we stopped using the word *baby* in front of little Zack's name. He's not a baby anymore. He said we are to call him Zachary."

The women smiled and the children surrounding them grinned at Zachary and each other.

Tommy ran over to Baby Zack and hit his chest with his hand. "You're Zachary."

Baby Zack grinned. "Me—Zachary, me—Zachary," he said and jumped up and down. "Zachary. . .Zachary. . . Zachary. . .

The children jumped up and down with him and yelled "Zachary. . .Zachary."

Everyone joined their tinkling laughter.

Allena picked up Zachary's hand. "Now I think it is time we all headed for home. . .but—" she turned and

looked at Mary Lou. "Now that Lars, Wilmot, and Genevieve are with Lily, Zachary misses his playmates and
gets lonesome. I'd like to take the twins home with me
so they can play together."

Mary Lou nodded. "Fine. When you're ready to eat
dinner, send them home."

"Oh, let them stay." Allena said and smiled down at
the children.

Mary Lou's glance met two pairs of upturned, implor-
ing eyes and threw her hands up. "Oh, all right, but come
home right after supper so you can get your chores
done."

The twins were off and running before her sentence
finished. Mary Lou watched everyone go, Laura swaying
in that familiar gait. It would be her turn soon. Mary Lou
sent a prayer to the Lord to bless Laura and Nelson with
a baby with a healthy body. For Nelson's sake. Although
she never mentioned it, she knew Allena was concerned.
His mother longed for Nelson to have a perfect child to
validate himself. They would know soon. Laura's baby
was carrying low.

fifteen

Mary Lou shaded her eyes and watched the twins run toward the main ranchhouse. Lars and Wilmot emerged from the barn to meet them, followed by Zachary. They all giggled then disappeared back into the barn. Mary Lou grinned. Her little daughter ran double time to keep up with the boys. With a sigh, she placed her hand on her stomach and wondered if a little sister resided within. She hoped so. Being surrounded with boys, Beth needed a girl to play girl's things with once in a while.

Following the sound of a hammer, Mary Lou went to see the new horse stalls Tom was building. The sun blazed a bright path through the barn from the open door. The horses were out to pasture so stalls were clean and empty except for Dulcie's. She stepped inside and rubbed her hands over her old friend's back and neck. Dulcie whinnied a welcome, swung her nose, and nuzzled Mary Lou's hand, hoping for a little tidbit. Mary Lou smoothed her velvety nose and pulled out a handful of sugar cubes from her apron pocket.

Dulcie nickered and happily gathered them off her palm with her soft lips. Mary Lou patted her friend's neck and ran her hands down to Dulcie's left front foot. She had stepped on a sharp thistle when they were out riding a couple days ago, and it had made a puncture on the back of her lower leg. Mary Lou lifted her hoof to see how it was healing. It looked good. Another couple days and it should be almost healed.

A moan and a soft whimper froze Mary Lou to the spot. She stood still, held her breath, and listened. All was quiet. The sound seemed to have come from one of the empty stalls down about three or four from where she stood. It had sounded human. . .

Mary Lou took a deep breath to slow her pounding heart and quietly made her way to the stall she thought the sound had come from. She approached slowly and peeked over the edge of the stall. Nothing there. She tried the next one.

There in a corner someone lay curled up and half covered with straw. What was someone doing here? Where had he come from? Quietly, Mary Lou opened the stall door just enough to let her slide through. She didn't want to startle the intruder nor did she want to alert him for fear he would get away.

A small person lay on one side, face turned away from her, almost lost in a large pair of boy's pants and an equally large flannel shirt. Long, blond, straight hair covered his shoulders like a shawl. Could it be a girl? Where had she come from and what on earth was she doing here alone in their barn? Mary Lou didn't want to startle or frighten her. She said, "Hello," as quietly and cheerfully as she could.

The girl rolled over, gasped, jumped to her feet, and pressed her back against the wall. She cowered like a frightened animal, her arms out in front for protection. Her wide eyes spoke fear and darted up, down, around the stall and out the door, searching for a way of escape.

Mary Lou held out her hand and smiled. "It's all right, child. I'm not going to hurt you. I'm a mother and I know how frightened a girl can be." She walked slowly toward her.

The young girl's eyes darted desperately for a way of

escape. She must have fallen somewhere because her whole left sleeve was torn, her arm bruised, badly scraped, and caked with dried blood.

"Oh, you're hurt." Mary Lou reached out her hand. "Come, child, let's go up to the house so I can clean your arm and put some salve and a bandage on it."

The girl didn't move or make a sound. Her eyes reflected her inner terror.

"I'm Mary Lou Langdon and this is our ranch. It's all right if you want to use the hay mow to sleep in if you are passing through."

A pair of suspicious eyes flashed doubt.

Mary Lou extended her hand again. "Honest, I won't hurt you. I have a little girl of my own, and if my little girl was lost I would hope some kind person would help her." Mary Lou walked toward her. "Oh my, your arm is bleeding and needs to be bandaged."

Mary Lou reached to touch her.

The girl ducked and raised a protective arm over her face.

This child acts as if she has been beaten and abused, Mary Lou thought. She slowly walked forward. "Come, dear, I won't hurt you. I just want to help you. You need your arm salved and bandaged." Mary Lou offered her hand. "Come with me and I'll take care of it."

The girl's fearful eyes grew confused.

"Are you hungry?" Mary Lou knew by the change of expression on her face she had finally hit a responsive chord. She held out her hand.

The girl ducked and cowered as if waiting to be struck.

"Please believe me when I tell you I won't hurt you, dear," Mary Lou assured her. "I want to help you. When did you eat last? If you slept here last night, I'm sure you must be hungry. Come, take my hand so we can walk to the house, or follow me if you'd rather."

The girl's suspicious eyes searched Mary Lou's face for a long moment. Then she hesitantly lifted her hand and placed it in Mary Lou's.

"Good. Come, now let's see what we can find to eat to fill you up."

As they walked together toward the house, the girl's eyes darted like an alert rabbit at the slightest movement anywhere.

When Mary Lou opened the door to go into the kitchen the girl hesitated.

"Come, my dear, there isn't any one here right now. Just the two of us." Mary Lou dropped her hand and walked into the house.

Slowly the girl edged through the door and plastered herself against the inside wall right beside it.

Mary Lou went to the breadbox and took out a loaf of bread, put a few pieces of cheese on a plate, poured a glass of milk, and set them on the table. She smiled at the girl and pulled out a chair. "Come and sit, child, while I pour us a cup of tea."

The girl walked slowly and perched on the chair's edge, one leg positioned to leap and run. She grabbed a piece of cheese in one hand and a slice of bread in the other and tried to stuff them into her mouth all at once.

"It's all right, my dear, you don't have to eat fast. No one will take it away from you. You're safe here."

Mary Lou dished out some of her canned peaches and placed them in front of her.

The girl's eyes followed Mary Lou's every move while she continued to stuff the food in her mouth and chew as fast as possible.

"My husband and our little boy and girl will be here

before long for dinner. You can stay and eat again with us, if you like. I have stew cooking on the stove."

The young girl relaxed a bit yet gobbled the food, still darting quick glances back as she ate, as if someone were going to snatch it from her.

Mary Lou replaced the teakettle on the stove and pretended not to notice the girl stuff bits of food in her pockets. Where had this girl come from? Mary Lou guessed she was fifteen or sixteen. She didn't recognize her or remember ever having seen her anywhere in town or on the ranches in these parts. Perhaps after she felt safer, she might talk a bit and tell something about herself.

As she ate, Mary Lou noticed her gradually begin to relax and smiled at her. "Now that you feel better with a full tummy can you tell me your name and where you came from?" She had begun to wonder if the girl could speak.

A buggy rumbled up the lane and into the yard. Mary Lou rose and walked to the door. It was Lily.

The girl jumped up from the table, grabbed and stuffed as much bread and cheese as she could into her pockets, and got ready to bolt.

Mary Lou grabbed her. "Oh! No, child. You don't need to be afraid of Lily. She's my sister-in-law. She won't hurt you." Mary Lou dragged her to the door, held her tight, and let her look out.

Lily climbed down from her buggy.

The girl cowered and wiggled but Mary Lou held her tight. Lily opened the door and walked in. "What—?"

"I found this young girl in our barn this morning. She's hungry and very frightened. I'm glad you came." Mary Lou spoke into the girl's ear, "Lily won't hurt you or tell anyone you are here, I promise you. We'll both help you."

Lily quickly sized up the situation and wisely sat down in a chair.

Mary Lou guided the girl back to the table, released her into a chair, and stood behind with her hands over the girl's shoulders.

Lily looked at her and smiled. "Hello. "I'm Lily and I promise you, I won't hurt you or even tell them you are here."

The girl's eyes widened with fear and darted all directions for a way of escape.

"Lily! You know her?"

"Not really, but I was in Harness today and paid a visit to the girls at the brothel and heard a big fuss about a new girl who had run away."

The girl uttered a fearful cry, shot up out of the chair, and bolted for the door.

Lily beat her to it, caught her, and determinedly hung on while the girl flayed, squirmed, and fought to free herself. "Be still, child," Lily said. "We want to help you get away from that place."

The girl looked up into Lily's face in disbelief then threw her arms around Lily and sobbed.

Lily held her tight then slowly walked her to the couch and sat down beside her. When the girl's sobs quieted, Lily cupped her face in her hands, kissed her on both cheeks, then looked at Mary Lou. "I went into Harness for supplies this morning. I hadn't been to the brothel for a while, so I thought I would pay the girls a visit." She looked into the young girl's terrified eyes. "I used to live there, child. Did anyone mention Lily?"

The wide-eyed girl shook her head.

"I don't live there anymore. Now I go to visit the girls. to tell them about the freedom they could have in

Jesus. Today they told me that a new young girl had come into the house three days ago and had escaped and run away during the night."

The girl's interest turned to terror, and she leaped to her feet. "No! I won't go back! I won't! I can't!" Her wild eyes searched the room for a place to run. Suddenly she turned and bolted for the door.

Lily leaped, grabbed her, and hung on until she quit struggling. "Be quiet, child! Quit fighting me. We are not going to force you to go back there. It's another kind of slavery. We want to help you get back home to your parents."

The girl stopped struggling, looked up into Lily's face in unbelief, threw her arms around her, and dissolved into tears. "Oh. . .thank you. . .thank you," she cried and clung.

Lily held her, stroked her long, blond hair and let her cry. When her sobs quieted, Lily asked, "Where do you live, and where did you think you were going when you came away with the man who brought you here?"

"I live in Jordan, Missouri, and my mother and I answered an ad in our newspaper for a nanny. A man called and told us the job was in Belleville, which is about forty miles from my home. The man had papers and references, a picture of the family and the three children I would care for. My father finally gave his consent for me to take the job. We left and drove about six hours till we came to a hotel, then—" The girl burst into tears and covered her face.

Lily folded the girl into her arms, closed her eyes and prayed. *O God, our Father, thank You for sending your child to us for protection. We know when we do Your will we also move under Your protection. Thank You, Father, for the privilege of serving You. And since You have sent her to us, Lord, we know You will also guide us and show us the way to save her from this awful evil that is trying to snatch away her life. I vow, Father, to do everything I can to protect her until You show us Your will to get her back to her own family. In Jesus' name, Amen.*

Lily turned to Mary Lou, her eyes swimming with tears. "I am going to give this young girl the opportunity I longed for, in thanks to Doug for saving me out of that pit of hell." A glow seemed to emanate from Lily's face. "You know, Mary Lou," Lily said softly, "God has even taught me to thank Him for Doug. When Doug married me I knew it was only for his own selfish purposes, but I had my own reasons in marrying him. I used him to escape the brothel. It's too bad Doug never realized what he did for me in giving me the gift of his family and Genevieve. The Bible says, 'he meant it for evil but God meant it for good.' Doug also taught me our heaven or hell begins here on earth, and we choose which one we want to live in."

Lily's confession lifted Mary Lou's heart to thanksgiving, and she joined Lily in a joyous prayer to God for His saving grace.

The girl listened in awe. "You're Christians!"

"Yes, we are," Lily said. "Do you come from a Christian family? Are you a Christian?

"Yes."

"Then you are our sister in Christ." Lily cupped the girl's face and looked seriously into her eyes. "I want you to listen very carefully to what I say and what I want you to do, because it is the only way we can protect you and get you back to your own family. Will you give me your promise you'll do what I tell you?"

The girl's wide eyes sparkled with fresh tears. She

nodded and whispered, "Yes."

Lily glanced at Mary Lou. "Could she stay at your house and you keep her out of sight after we contact her family? I'm afraid if I took her home they might come looking for her there. It's just a wild guess, but I think she'll be safer with you."

Mary Lou nodded and turned to the girl. "I promise you will be as safe here with me as you would be at Lily's, because we're family."

"Now, tell me your name, where you came from and if your folks have a telephone?"

"Yes, we do. My name is Isobel Henderson, and my father is George William Henderson. We live in Elk Hill, Arkansas, and our phone number is 3542."

"We'll have to go down to the main ranch house to use the new telephone," Lily said, "but you needn't be afraid. Our whole family will protect you."

The three walked to the main ranch.

Lily introduced Isobel to Allena and Hattie, who were curious about the stranger, but Lily didn't seem inclined to give any details. "We need to use the telephone to call this girl's father so he can come get her and take her back home."

Both Allena's and Hattie's eyebrows raised in question but they kept mum.

Lily placed the call with the local operator, and they all sat and waited till she called back. When the phone rang three longs and two shorts Lily rushed to the telephone. "Hello, Mr. George Henderson? This is Lily Langdon. You don't know me but I live in Harness, Texas, and your daughter, Isobel, is beside me and wants to talk to you." Lily handed Isobel the phone.

Isobel smiled and grabbed the receiver. "Papa?"

"Isobel! We've been wondering about you. You said

you would call us as soon as you got to your new job. We didn't hear from you and were getting worried. But you're there safe and sound. Good. How is the job? Is it what you hoped it would be?" Her father shouted into the phone as if he had to shout across the miles.

Mary Lou, Lily and Allena heard him plainly.

"Well, Papa, no, it isn't. . .exactly what I wanted, and I want to come home." Isobel looked in bewilderment at Lily, her lips trembled.

Lily took the phone. "Mr. Henderson? This is Lily Langdon. I'm a new friend of Isobel and want you to know she is safe here with our family."

"Safe? What do you mean 'safe'?" Mr. Ryan asked. "Is my daughter all right? Let me talk to her."

Lily handed the phone back to Isobel. "Your father wants to talk to you."

"Papa?" Isobel's voice broke. "Papa, the job—was—was not the right job for me." She fought tears.

"Are you all right?"

"Oh, yes, Papa, I'm fine now that I hear your voice. . . I—uh—guess I'm just homesick. I miss you and mama and my brothers so much. I got to thinking—maybe—I'd be better off if I come home and take the job in Mrs. Landeau's millinery shop for a while. I know one thing, Papa, I want to find a job close to home." She swallowed her tears.

Lily put her arm around the girl.

"Papa, Mrs. Williams wants to talk to you. They are a wonderful family who took me in—ah—when I didn't have any place to stay. And they are Christians, Papa. They live on a great big Texas ranch!"

"A Texas ranch! How on earth did you ever get to Texas?"

"Oh—Papa—I'll tell you all about it when I get home.

It would cost too much to tell you over the phone." Isobel handed the phone to Lily, smiled through her tears, and backed away.

Lily took the receiver and gave Mr. Henderson directions to get to Harness by train and the Langdon phone number to call from the station when he arrived. "We will gladly meet you there."

"Her older brother and I will be on the next train to Harness, Texas. Good-bye—and—thank you for your hospitality to my daughter. God bless you."

Lily grinned as she hooked the receiver in its place and put her arm around Isobel. "There. You'll be back home safe and sound before you know it." Lily stood looking at her. Suddenly her mouth dropped open. "Wait a minute—I think we had better call you by another name. *Isobel* is an unusual name. Word of mouth travels fast around here and I don't know of any other *Isobel* in these parts."

"How about *Grace*?" Mary Lou suggested. "It is by the grace of God, Isobel, you are here, and calling you 'Grace' will remind us we are all doing the Lord's work, but nobody else will be the wiser."

Isobel looked at the four women surrounding her, and her eyes welled with tears. "How am I ever going to thank you all? May the Lord bless you greatly for saving me from—" Her lips couldn't form the words. "I shall never forget to pray for you and ask the Lord to bless you always."

Mary Lou and Isobel walked back to her house. As they neared, the children came running from the barn and Tommy hollered, "Is it supper time yet?"

"Almost," his mother answered.

"Incidentally, out of sheer curiosity, where did you get the boy's clothes you have on?" Mary Lou asked.

Grace smiled. "Off a clothesline. I should return them. I didn't mean to steal them—but I had to have some different clothes or I would have stood out like a sore thumb."

The women laughed.

A beautiful smile transformed Grace's worried face and her eyes grew moist. She stopped and looked up into the sky. "Thank You. Thank You, dear God." She looked at Mary Lou. "And thank You, God, for sending two of your angels in answer to my prayers."

Mary Lou smiled and said, "Amen."

sixteen

Tom, Lily, and Mary Lou, her arm around Isobel, watched the train pull to a clanking, wheezing, stop.

The conductor hung on the bottom step of the passenger car till it slowed, hopped off, and placed the stepstool for passengers to disembark.

A tall, distinguished gentleman and a handsome, young red-headed boy as tall as his father stepped down.

"Papa!" Isobel cried and flew to the welcome arms of her father, who flashed a broad, relieved smile, folded her into them, then held her back and stared at her. "Are you all right?"

"Yes, Papa." She turned to her brother and smiled. "Hello, Freddie," she said softly. Their eyes held for a moment, and Freddie stepped forward and put his arms around her. "You all right, Sis?" he asked.

She smiled big and turned to the Langdons. "Father, Freddie, this is Tom and Mary Lou Langdon and Lily Williams who have been so kind to me."

Mr. Henderson shook Tom's hand heartily and bowed to the ladies. "My eternal thanks to you for your kindness and hospitality to my daughter. I must admit I was leery of my daughter going off by herself to an out-of-town job." He turned to Isobel and frowned. "But how on earth did you get way down here in Texas?"

Isobel laughed. "Oh, Papa, it's a long story and I'll tell you all about it as we ride back home."

"You have a wonderful daughter, Mr. Henderson," Mary Lou said quickly and smiled at Isobel. "She was a brave girl to venture out to discover like most of us that sometimes there is no place like home, where the love is."

Isobel's relieved smile flashed her thanks.

Tom led the way to the buggies. "I learned from the station master that your return train will leave here at eleven tomorrow morning. We'd be right happy to have you stay at our ranch overnight. Then we can bring you in to meet the train tomorrow," Tom offered.

"That is very kind of you, sir. I am in your debt."

Tom nodded. "My pleasure, sir." Tom loaded the men's suitcase in the back of the wagon as the men climbed aboard.

The ladies got into Mary Lou's buggy and led off to put some dust distance between them.

Lily glanced at Isobel. "May I say that it would be better for you and your whole family if this whole trip would be forgotten. The least said is always the easiest mended."

Isobel nodded. "I'm glad you said that, Lily. I was wondering what I should do. It would break Papa and Mama's heart if I told them, and I've put them through enough grief already." Isobel glanced from Lily to Mary Lou, and her eyes filled with tears. "I'll never forget either of you or your kindness to me." She pulled her handkerchief from her sleeve. "My grandma always says "God never leaves his children unattended." Isobel looked toward heaven. "I'm so thankful—"

"Your grandmother sounds like she's well acquainted with our Father in heaven. We're happy you're going home safe and sound." Lily laughed. "Surely you have a nice young man who has been watching you grow up and has claimed you for his own, haven't you?"

Isobel blushed and lowered her eyes. "Yes."

"Good." Lily lifted her face and kissed her cheek. "Marry him as soon as he asks you, and God bless you both."

After one of Hattie's delicious dinners, Tom, Tex, Mr. Henderson, and Freddie mounted horses and rode around the barns and out on the range and viewed cattle grazing as far as they could see.

Mr. Henderson and his son were noticeably impressed. "My, you have quite a sizeable ranch here." After the tour, they returned to the main ranch and sat on the porch. "Back east, we hear so much about the Chisholm trail. Is it true that cattlemen drive their cattle over six hundred miles north to the railroad at Abilene, Kansas, to ship them east? Do you use that trail?"

Tom grinned. "We used to but now that the railroads are being built in Texas we ship our cattle north by rail if we can. We fare better that way. As a businessman would you rather receive four dollars a head for cattle in Texas or forty dollars a head in Chicago?"

"That much difference?" Mr. Henderson nodded his head.

"Oh, yes." Tom grinned. "When we trailed them, it used to cost about a dollar a head to move a normal-size herd of 2,500, moving an average ten to fifteen miles a day."

Mr. Henderson nodded and grinned. "Very interesting. Like all young boys, I had my dreams of going west and becoming a cowboy but ended up being a businessman like my father."

The ladies walked onto the porch.

Talk gradually ceased and finally everyone said good night and were directed to a bed with a promise of an early morning call so everyone could get breakfast before they left for Harness.

The next morning Hattie outdid herself with a generous Texas breakfast which drew much praise from Mr. Henderson.

"I'm afraid if I ate this amount of good cooking every day I'd scarce be able to rise from my chair. It is delicious, madam."

Hattie smiled and blushed.

At nine-thirty, Tom brought Allena's big buggy around. They went down to the main ranch to pick up Lily and Isobel. Lily had been delighted to have Isobel's company for the night. They both boarded. Tom turned the buggy toward Harness.

The train tooted from afar and finally rumbled into the station and halted. The conductor hopped off and placed the step stool. "All aboard in ten minutes," as he called walked toward the station.

Lily and Mary Lou hugged Isobel.

"Please write once in a while to let us know how you are," Mary Lou requested.

Lily nodded in agreement. "We want to know when you find that nice young man you want to marry."

Isobel blushed. "I think I might do what Mama wanted me to do. She was a schoolteacher and wanted me to be one. My papa said he'd send me to normal school if I want to become one."

"My mama was a schoolteacher too, before she married Pa," Mary Lou said wistfully.

"All aboard!"

Isobel clung to Mary Lou and Lily. "Thank you. God bless you both for saving me from a life worse than death."

Lily kissed both her cheeks. Isobel's father handed her up into the steps and her brother followed.

Mr. Henderson turned to Mary Lou and Lily. "I am

indebted to you ladies for your care and concern for my daughter. God bless you." He bowed his head and turn and swung up the train steps.

As the train slowly rolled away, Isobel pressed against the window and waved and was gone.

seventeen

Mary Lou smiled with pride as she watched her energetic twins run down the road to the main ranch, Beth's long curls bouncing, her skirt flapping around her legs. As usual, Beth was trying to keep up with Tommy.

Suddenly, Beth stopped, turned, ran back, took her mother's hand, and walked like a little lady beside her. Mary Lou glanced down into her upturned face and smiled.

"Tommy just wants to hurry and play with the boys, but we walk like ladies, don't we, Mama?"

Mary Lou suppressed a smile. "Yes, we do, Beth."

Beth nodded her head emphatically. "We walk like ladies," she repeated and fell into step with her mother, who narrowed her steps to fit the little five-year-old lady beside her.

Mary Lou had often wondered what Mama had looked like when she was a little girl. She had no pictures of Mama as a child but could see many of Mama's mannerisms in Beth, and her daughter had Mama's eyes and hair.

For a while, Mary Lou had despaired that her dainty little Beth would become a tomboy. Considering the fact that most of her playmates were boys, it should have come as no surprise. But lately Beth had quieted some, and she often came into the house by herself to play with her doll, or she brought a book to Mary Lou to read to her, rather than play with the boys. Now Mary Lou had begun to share whatever task she was into, and Beth seemed to enjoy working with her. After supper, Mary Lou and Beth did the supper dishes together while Tom and Tommy went out to the barn to do evening chores.

As they approached the main ranch, Genevieve came running out the door, waved, and ran toward them.

"Geevie, Geevie," Beth called and raced to meet her.

When they met they grabbed hands, giggled, and wandered off into their own little world of fantasy.

Mary Lou walked into an empty kitchen. It was unusual not to find Hattie bustling about her work. All seemed strangely quiet.

"Hello!" Mary Lou called.

"Hello!" The answer came from one of the bedrooms.

She found Nelson in his wheelchair in the hall outside his bedroom door, with a worried look on his face.

A painful moan came from within.

Mary Lou leaned over and patted Nelson's shoulder and smiled. "When did all this start?" she asked.

"About five this morning."

"Mary Lou? That you? Come in here!" Allena called from the bedroom.

Mary Lou hurried in.

Laura lay on her bed, tossing her head and pulling the side of the mattress against the pain. In a relaxed moment Laura gave Mary Lou a weak smile.

Mary Lou leaned over and gave her a quick kiss on a damp forehead, smoothed her hair back, and smiled. "I'm glad your time is here. I know I'll be glad when mine is. Just keep thinking that the reason for the pain is so that little baby who is giving you so much trouble now will soon be resting in your arms."

Laura's mouth hinted at a smile. She blinked her eyes and nodded agreement. Then another pain began its course.

"Good, Mary Lou, you came just at the right time," Allena said without looking up. "Get washed."

Mary Lou washed her hands and hurried back to the bedside. "What's happening?"

"The baby is in good position," Allena said. "It shouldn't be too long now."

Laura held the sides of her stomach, taking short, shallow breaths and blowing them out, then suddenly moaned, inhaled, and grabbed Mary Lou's arm and pulled as another pain began.

Hattie came in with a fresh basin of hot water and plenty of cloths and set them on the commode, walked to the bedside, and felt Laura's forehead and her stomach. "You've dropped quite a bit, child. We should have this little tyke in our arms before long."

Laura stretched a weak, thankful smile and drawled, "I'm willin'—anytime!" She relaxed a bit, then another pain started its course.

"When did her pains begin?" Mary Lou asked Allena.

"Early this morning, and the way this baby's moving, it looks like it's in a hurry to get here. I don't think it will be too long now."

Allena was right. One-half hour after those words, she gave a sound smack to the tiny buttocks of a baby boy with two perfect, strong legs, who gasped for his first breath of Texas air and let out a husky squeal.

Mary Lou hurried out to Nelson, sitting right outside the door, grabbed him by the shoulders, and beamed at him. "Nelson! You have a son—a beautiful, perfect baby boy."

Nelson took a deep breath, closed his eyes, and exhaled. "Thank God," he said. "How's Laura?"

"Oh, she's fine and mighty proud to give you a son."

Nelson bent his head over his chest.

Mary Lou put her arms around him. He was trembling. She knew she could never imagine the deep concern he must have had, wondering if his child would be whole and healthy. *Thank You, Father, for Your sweet graciousness to Nelson and Laura. Thank You for that whole, healthy baby boy, for a son who will make them proud someday.*

Shortly, Allena walked out of the bedroom with her new grandson in her arms and gently placed him in Nelson's lap. "You hold your son for a bit while his mother takes a well-earned rest." She opened the blanket and bared a squirming little fellow with two strong, little legs kicking the air. "All right, Papa, what are you going to name him?"

Nelson's face beamed. He slowly ran his hands over each perfectly formed limb, then folded the blanket over him and gathered his son into his arms and held his small body against his chest. He looked up with glistening eyes. "His name is *Jonathan,* 'Jehovah has given'."

Tears would not stay contained and spilled down Mary Lou's cheeks. "He is a beautiful boy." At last, Nelson had found his fulfillment as a man in his perfect little son. She patted his shoulder and smiled at Allena. "Congratulations, Grandma." She knew it was just as big a victory for Allena.

Now it was time for Mary Lou to gather her twins and go home, where chores too numerous to count were piled sky high, awaiting her.

A horse galloped into the yard.

Mary Lou looked out he window. It was Tom on his way to town. He dismounted, ground-reined Tinder, and hurried into the house. She met him at the door and took him immediately to Nelson's bedroom without saying a word.

Tom grinned. "Well, little brother, what have we here?"

Nelson's broad smile sparked a twinkle in his eye. "We have my son—my perfectly healthy son." He leaned over and picked him up from Laura's side, laid him gently on his lap, and unwrapped the blanket to expose two active, jerking little legs. When Nelson looked up at Tom, there were tears in his eyes.

Tom gripped his shoulder, grabbed his hand, and squeezed it hard. "I'm glad, Nelson. I'm happy for you." He glanced at Laura. "For you both."

Mary Lou thought for the thousandth time since she had become a Langdon how wonderful it was to have brothers and sisters. "The Lord supplieth our every need," Mama had often said. He certainly had for her. She left Tom with Nelson and walked back to the kitchen. She felt her Aunt Nelda's letter in her apron pocket, the one she had picked up from the mailbox. Her aunt had mentioned again that they were making plans to visit within the month and would come by train.

An old thought Mary Lou had nurtured for a long time surfaced again. Maybe after they got here and saw Texas they might consider moving to live with her, Tom, and the children. Pa would love being around all the horses and his grandchildren. . .they could bring all of Mama's things.

She'd talk to Tom.

eighteen

Beth, dressed and ready for school, sat quietly at the kitchen table, eating her oatmeal.

Mary Lou gathered the twins' lunches into their tin buckets and set them on the chair beside the door. "Tommy," she called, "come eat your breakfast!"

Tommy bounced into the kitchen, plopped on a chair, and began eating. "Do I have to stay at school all day, Mama?"

"Till two o'clock. Today, Grandma Langdon and I will be there to get you and bring you home. Now, sit down and eat your breakfast."

Tommy shoved a spoonful of oatmeal into his mouth. "What we gonna do at school, Mama?"

Mary Lou smiled. Tommy always had to "do" something, which to him meant action. The confinement of sitting at a desk most of the day would be hard for him. "I don't know exactly what Miss Truesdale or Miss Whitney will be teaching today, but you'll learn your numbers and how to read and write. Now, eat your oatmeal before it gets cold."

"I know my numbers, Mama, one, two, three, four, five, six, seven, eight, nine, ten." A proud grin spread across his little face.

"That's good, Tommy, but it's only the beginning. There are lots more numbers than just the ones you know, for instance, three hundred and eighty-five and six thousand twelve." She glanced at Tommy, whose spoon of oatmeal paused midair. "And you'll learn to write your letters and read a book. Wait and see. There will be a lots of other things to do at school, too. Right now eat your oatmeal."

Mary Lou and Tom both knew no amount of talking would ever convince Tommy that school would be better for him than staying on the ranch to work with his father. Tom had proudly said he was a good little worker.

"I like school." Beth said and nodded assurance. "You're gonna like school, too, Tommy."

Tommy frowned, but thought about it as he slowly ate his oatmeal. "I like school," he said slowly, then looked up. "But I should be here. Papa needs me."

It seemed nothing anyone said about school had yet convinced Tommy it was worth leaving his Papa. The only reason he was going was because his Papa had said he must.

When the children finished eating, Mary Lou handed them their drawstring schoolbags with a pencil and a writing tablet in each and their lunch buckets. They walked to the barn.

Tom saw them coming and raised his eyebrows in surprise at his neat little son. Tom grinned and winked at Mary Lou, and the four of them climbed aboard the wagon.

Tom snapped the reins to move the team, leaned toward Mary Lou, and said softly, "I don't think I quite convinced him yesterday that I could get along without him."

Mary Lou smiled. In a way she was glad. It had always pleased her that Tommy felt it such an honor to work with his father. When you have a good father, what better place to learn to become a good man yourself? Mary Lou's heart flooded with thanksgiving to God for another blessing.

Allena had announced today as canning day for tomatoes and corn. Mary Lou would spend the day at the main ranch until the children came home from school. Mary Lou had packed her jars early and put them in Tommy's little pull wagon. As always, when the women canned, Jess fed all the men from the chuck wagon at the main ranch.

Zack was sitting at the kitchen table finishing his breakfast when Mary Lou and Tom entered the ranch kitchen.

Tom patted a welcome on his brother's shoulder. "I didn't know you were home. I'm glad you can go with me."

"The legislature adjourned for a month to give the men a chance to go home for harvest. That worked fine for me. I wanted to be here to take Zachary to his first day of school and get my new office set up in Harness. I hear you're taking the kids. Good, I'll tie Victor to the wagon and ride with you."

Finally, all were ready, and the fathers and children rode off.

Mary Lou waved her hand over her head and smiled but couldn't suppress a tinge of sadness skirting her feelings of joy. Her children were no longer babies. Their first five years had flown by. Her feelings were mixed. She was relieved and looked forward to a bulk of uninterrupted time each day to get more work done as the child within grew more active. She placed her hands on her stomach and lifted her face to the sky. *Thank you, Father, for this child. They are babies such a short while.* She wondered if her Father in heaven was as eager to see his children grow up as we humans are.

As the wagon rolled away with the children, Mary

Lou waved away their babyhood in a strange mixture of feelings.

Tom pulled the wagon into the schoolyard, looked over at Zack, and grinned. Nostalgia flooded him. They had gone to this same one-room school when they were boys, and Miss Whitney had stood in the same place at the schoolhouse door as she did now.

Sarah Whitney met them and welcomed their boys with a big smile. "Well, well," she said, "and here come two of my favorite pupils now grown into fathers. I hope your sons are just like you."

Tom grinned. "Is that good or bad, Miss Whitney?"

"Why good! Both of you were bright little boys and did your lessons well. Zachary was a serious student but—" she looked at Tom and smiled. "I must say this, Tom, you were a good student but also particularly good at finding mischief to get into."

Tom ducked his head and laughed. "I'm afraid you're right, Miss Whitney, and if my son is like me and gives you any trouble, just let me know."

Miss Whitney frowned and shook her head. "If I could handle you, I think Miss Truesdale and I can handle one good, little, rambunctious boy."

At precisely eight-thirty, Miss Truesdale stepped out of the school door, stood on the top step and rang the school bell. "Children! Form a line," she called.

The children halted in their tracks. The older students hurried to follow orders and raced to get in line. Zachary and Tommy hesitated for a moment then followed a couple other boys and stood in line. Miss Whitney waved her hand at a few stragglers and they hustled.

Miss Truesdale stood ramrod straight. "Children, when you come into the schoolroom, put your lunch buckets on the shelves under the first window at the back and then sit down in any seat. I will give everyone his permanent seat later and no talking, please."

Zack watched his son follow the orders. He and Zachary had a good talk yesterday on how to behave in school. This morning they had discussed school manners and obeying the teacher. Zachary had shown a strong inclination to want to learn his letters and numbers so Zack had taught him as much as he could when he was home and discovered his son had a quick mind. Now he would see what Miss Truesdale could do with him.

As Miss Truesdale glanced toward him as she turned to follow her students into the schoolhouse, Zack tipped his hat to her.

She smiled, gave a quick nod, and disappeared into the classroom.

Zack watched till she disappeared. He could now admit he had admired her from the first day he met her. She was a lady. He untied Victor from Tom's wagon, mounted, and rode off toward Harness.

Tom waved his hat over his head and turned his wagon toward the Circle Z.

Zack saluted Tom then let Victor pick his own pace. He needed time to think. Before he met Darcy his plans had been to establish his own law office in Harness then perhaps reach for the state legislature. Once married, all his plans had been set aside. As far as Darcy and her father were concerned, there had been no other course than for him to go into his father-in-law's law firm. Zack decided now was the time to pick up his dreams, capitalize on the law experience he had gained in Boston, and aim for the Texas state legislature sooner than he had originally planned. There was only one thing that bothered him. After Darcy's death, he had seen a change in his son. When Zack was home his son followed him around, and he clung to him when he left. Now within a month he planned to leave again to attend the legislative session to lay some groundwork.

He and his mother would have to have a talk. She had raised three sons, and Zachary was her charge when he wasn't home. Right now, Zack needed a woman's input. He would talk to his mother tonight.

nineteen

With the twins in school, Mary Lou finished her morning chores early and slowly walked to the main ranch mailbox. The sun hung high and hot, but its golden head was shaded by large, cottony clouds that had lingered in the sky for several days, growing heavier and darker. The poor, dry, dusty earth stretched its arms for a drink.

With most of the crops harvested and the bulk of the canning done, Mary Lou felt done in. Her body drooped like a heavy sack and her back had been aching for a couple days. She was more than ready to have this baby. To have her slim body and energy back to work for her would be wonderful.

She walked slowly. June, their new shepherd collie dog, caught up with her and trotted alongside. Mary Lou patted her head. "Poor pup. You miss your morning romp with the twins, don't you?" Mary Lou laughed. "Sorry, June. I'm not up to much more than a lean over to pat your head."

A sharp pain shot through her back and took her breath. That was the hardest one yet. She had been having pains off and on all morning. Should she turn and go back home? She stopped and took a deep breath. The pain eased so she continued to the main ranch. If she needed help, it was closest.

Hattie stretched and hung a wet shirt on the line and spotted movement on the road to Tom's ranch. She shaded her eyes. Mary Lou was coming. She hung a few more shirts and looked for Mary Lou again. She had stopped and was standing, holding her stomach. Slowly she began to move then stopped again. Hattie turned from her clothesline and hurried into the house.

She emerged as quickly as she went in, followed by Lily, who shaded her eyes and watched Mary Lou walk unsteadily toward the ranch. "Hattie, keep your water boiling. I'm going to get Mary Lou." She ran to the ranch door and called. "Mother, come help me with Mary Lou!"

Lily was barely out the gate when Allena hurried through the kitchen door and followed her.

Mary Lou knew she was in trouble. The pains were stabbing not only her back but down near the bottom of her stomach. Her legs grew unsteady. She looked for something to hang on to. There was nothing. She put one foot in front of the other. She had to keep walking.

Active movement from the ranch put a smile of relief on her face, and she stopped. Lily and Allena were running toward her. She broke out in a cold sweat and staggered forward as best she could.

"We're coming Mary Lou," Allena called. "Just stand there."

Mary Lou stopped while another pain shot through her body. Ambivalent feelings of fear and joy moved one foot in front of the other, and she staggered forward. She was breathing hard. This baby was coming, ready or not! Lily and Allena were running toward her. She smiled and raised her face to heaven. "Thank You. . .Oh, thank You, Lord." Her knees became unreliable, and she was sinking to the ground when Lily and Allena reached her and caught her before she fell.

Allena picked her up like a baby and carried her back down to the ranch.

Lily hurried on ahead, calling, "Hattie, Hattie, get

things ready! Mary Lou's having her baby."

One pain blended into another until Mary Lou felt as if she were being torn apart; then she thankfully sank into oblivion while her body seemed to tear into a dozen pieces.

When she opened her eyes, she was in Allena's high four-poster bed. Her body was at peace, and Allena was sitting at her side, smiling at her. She felt her stomach. It was flat. She started to raise up. "The baby—"

"Lie back down and rest, my dear, your task is finished."

Allena said, rising up and tenderly kissing her forehead. "Thank you, Mary Lou, for giving me another granddaughter."

Mary Lou's smile spread from ear to ear. Inner joy overwhelmed her. God had answered her prayer for a baby sister for Beth. Now her whole being lifted in a wordless prayer of joy and thanksgiving.

Tom sat at the side of the bed, holding one of her hands against his cheek. He leaned over her and touched his warm lips to hers. "Thank you, darling, for our new daughter."

She nodded and tried to smile, but a wave of weariness washed over her. She had never felt so tired in all her life. Her eyes closed voluntarily, and she had no strength to pry them open while she felt herself slowly sink into nothingness.

An eternity later, Mary Lou opened her eyes and turned her head. Tom sat beside the bed, looking down and smiling at the little bundle in his arms. She saw wisps of soft brown hair on a tiny head surrounded by a blanket. She slowly turned on her side and reached for her daughter.

Tom looked at her and smiled. "You're awake." He

laid their new daughter in her mother's arms. "Thank you, dear wife, for another sweet little daughter." He grinned. "She looks like you must have looked at this size."

Mary Lou laughed. "Oh, Tom, how would you know?"

"Remember your mother's locket you keep in your dresser drawer? Isn't that picture you?"

Mary Lou had forgotten about that. It was the only picture she had of herself as a child. She'd have to look at it again.

Allena walked up behind Tom and placed her hands on his shoulders. "If I'm any judge of babies, she is a little Mary Lou." She leaned over and kissed her daughter-in-law's forehead. "In my old age, I am going to be surrounded by the little girls I yearned and prayed for half my life, thanks to you and Lily. When am I going to learn that when the Lord blesses, he always blesses abundantly!"

Lily peeked into the room and grinned. "You awake? There are a couple little people here who would like to see you." She stepped back and pulled Tommy and Beth into the room.

Beth hurried to the bedside with worried eyes and stretched out her arms to her mother who folded her into hers. "You sick, Mama?"

"Just for a little bit. Tomorrow I'll be much better."

For the first time in his young life, Tommy had nothing to say. He stood at the side of the bed and stared at his mama.

Mary Lou reached out her arms for Tommy, who made a jump for the bed but was caught by his father, who sat him gently on the edge.

Mary Lou could barely contain the joy bursting within. She looked from Beth to Tommy. "Did you see your new baby sister?"

Both of them nodded.

"Where's the brother baby?" Tommy asked.

There was a breathless pause then everyone laughed.

How could Mary Lou ever explain to him why there was only one baby when he and his sister had been two? Perhaps it was time for Tommy to learn that there are some questions even his parents had no answers for.

After everyone was gone, Mary Lou's soul lifted in praise and thanksgiving to God for their new little daughter, and she sank into a restful sleep.

Later, after Tom had put the twins to bed he slid in beside Mary Lou and took her hand in his and kissed her fingers.

They looked into each other eyes and found a love deeper than either had ever dreamed existed.

"Thank you, Mary Lou, for being the beautiful wife and mother you are," he said in a whisper.

She snuggled into his arms. "Tom, I never knew such happiness existed until I met you. Mama told me once she prayed every night for God to search out a good husband for me and bring us together. God answered her prayer abundantly in you, Tom."

Tom kissed her eyes and the tip of her nose and found her lips. "Sure am glad God found me," he said through the tilt of an impish grin.

Mary Lou stretched and kissed him. "Me, too." She relaxed in his arms. Her tired body felt at peace. It had done its job well and now in its weariness sank into the blessed peace and safety of her husband's arms.

twenty

Tom finished cleaning the last stall, grabbed the handles of the manure-filled wheelbarrow, wheeled it out, and dumped it on the mound. On his way back into the barn, he saw Mary Lou running toward him, waving something over her head. Had something happened? He dropped the handles and hurried toward her.

"They're coming! They're coming!" she shouted.

Tom opened his arms and caught his breathless wife, whose face radiated a joy he hadn't seen there for a while. Now her eyes danced in her beaming face.

"Guess what! Pa and Aunt Nelda are coming to visit next month!" She handed Tom the postcard.

Can visit in August. Will telephone details, it said.

Tom looked up and laughed at Mary Lou's beaming face. He was glad for her sake. He knew she had grown homesick to see her aunt and father from little comments she often made about them. Surrounded as he was by his family all the time, he could only imagine what it must be like to seldom see them at all.

Breathless, Mary Lou began. "I'm sure Mother has some extra blankets I could borrow and she has a—"

"Whoa!" Tom laughed. "Let's take it one step at a time!"

She chattered on, planning where they would sleep. "They won't believe how big Beth and Tommy have grown. I'm glad Pa and Aunt Nelda will finally get to meet Allena. Pa will be thrilled with the ranch and all the horses—"

Tom let her talk. Her eyes were bright and sparked the plans that germinated in her mind and tumbled out her mouth.

She reached up, threw her arms around him, and kissed him. "Oh, I'm so happy they're coming. I've missed them so." She burst into tears.

Tom held her and let her cry out all the years of yearning he knew had built up inside her.

"Well—" Mary Lou pushed herself from Tom's arms, picked up her apron, dried her tears, and grinned. "Well, enough of that!" She smoothed down her apron, stretched up and kissed Tom again, turned, and ran for the house.

Tom grinned and went back to his wheelbarrow, finished the barn work, and walked to the house. He passed the cabin he and Mary Lou had lived in their few years of married life, while they were building their home. Now they used it for wood and tool storage. It was still a solid three-room cabin and had a good fireplace.

A recurring thought took root. Would Buck ever consider coming to live in Texas? He knew that was what Mary Lou yearned for. Buck and Nelda could live in that cabin, and Mary Lou could have her family with her.

The more Tom thought about it the more pleased he was with the idea. He'd keep mum and feel Buck out first before he said anything to anyone else. Tom would like to know Buck as a friend. He sensed in him a strong pride that his injury had broken. Perhaps if Tom opened the door and invited him to become part of the Circle Z, his injured pride could heal and he would be able to enjoy life instead of resenting it. The more he thought about it, the more Tom liked the idea. He'd wait and talk to Buck and get his thinking on it. No sense stirring up the nest before they were ready for it.

Tom grinned, remembering Nelda's help when Tom and Mary Lou were married. She had been on his side from the beginning and had finally pulled it off so Mary Lou didn't marry Glenn. He would be ever grateful to both Nelda and Tibby for their meddling. Without those "meddlin' ladies," he would have lost the love of his life. Tom had no doubt in his mind Nelda would be delighted and move without a qualm, but it would be up to Buck to make the final decision. He'd wait. The timing would have to be right.

Mary Lou sat in her kitchen rocker, nursing little Nellena. She could hardly contain herself. It would be wonderful to see Pa and Aunt Nelda again. Now *her* family could take part in the life of her children. She sighed. *Family is so important.* An old thought resurfaced. *Would it—could it ever be possible for Pa and Aunt Nelda to sell out in Kansas and come to Texas to live on their ranch? Pa could watch his grandchildren grow—Aunt Nelda would be part of a family again. . .* Mary Lou smiled. Mama always said when you think and dream of the things you want, you smoothe a path for them to come. Lately, Mary Lou had been thinking a lot about Papa and Aunt Nelda coming to live with her and Tom. Now it was time to talk with Tom.

She looked down at the sweet baby in her arms and smoothed the soft brown hair on her head, so much like the color of her own. For the thousandth time, she wished Mama could have seen her grandchildren. She would have been a proud and wonderful grandmother.

Mary Lou's eyes filled with tears. She laid her head on the back of the chair, slowly rocked, and raised her eyes to heaven. "Oh, Mama," she whispered, "can you see your new granddaughter? We named her *Nellena* after Aunt Nelda, you, and Allena who have all guided me to become the woman I am." She gazed down at her sleeping baby, rose, and gently laid her in the cradle and stood looking at her.

Was it wishing or purely imagination that made her feel Mama's presence so strong? Regardless, she relished the moment and sent a prayer of grateful thanks heavenward.

twenty-one

The Reverend Milford folded his hands on the pulpit and bowed his head.

The congregation bowed for his closing prayer.

"Our Father, we thank You for this time of worship on this beautiful Sabbath day and ask Your blessing on all who have gathered here. We thank You for strength and health, for friends and family and for the bounties of this harvest season." He raised his hand in benediction. "Now may Thy Holy Spirit rest upon you and give you peace today and throughout this week. In Jesus' name, Amen."

Reverend Milford stepped from the pulpit and walked down the center aisle to stand at the door and shake hands with his congregation as they filed out.

Allena remained in her seat until the congregation had left then walked over to Ruthella as she began to close up the organ. "We would be happy if you and Sarah would come home with us and join us for Sunday dinner. We never have a chance to visit at church."

Ruthella nodded "Oh, thank you, we'd be delighted." She hurried to Sarah, who nodded her head and smiled at Allena.

The ride home was pleasant. The leaves were beginning to turn. As they rode under the *Circle Z*, a horse and rider galloped in from the opposite direction. It was Zack.

They waved. He saluted from the brim of his hat and rode behind them to the ranchhouse, dismounted, and came to help the ladies from the buggy.

"This is a pleasant surprise," he said as he helped Ruthella down.

"Yes, thank you." Ruthella smiled and mentally scolded her heart for banging its surprised pleasure.

"Didn't see you in church, this morning, young man," Sarah said. "Where were you?"

Zack smiled. Same old schoolteacher checking up on her boys to see that they went to church. "It was eleven-thirty when my train got in from the legislature, so I came on home." He escorted the ladies to the ranch house door and opened it.

His observant mother met them and pulled Sarah in. "Dinner won't be ready for a bit, Zack. This is the first time Ruthella has been here, so why don't you and Ruthella take a little walk to show her the ranch and work up an appetite while we finish? We'll send one of the children to let you know when it's ready."

"Sounds like a good idea to me." He turned to Ruthella and cupped her elbow in his hand. "Do you mind?"

"I'd be delighted. I've heard the Circle Z is one of the biggest ranches in Texas."

Zack smiled. "We can thank our father for that. He was a man of great vision."

Ruthella liked a man who spoke well of his father. Her mother had told her to always beware of any man who didn't speak well of his family.

They walked toward the corral.

"May I extend my sympathy to you?" Ruthella said softly. "I heard your wife passed away."

"Thank you. It was a blessing in disguise. She was so badly injured and so ill she would have been a complete invalid all her life and bound to a bed or wheelchair. She couldn't have handled that. She loved life, and it would have been utterly miserable for her to have to live that way."

They walked around the vegetable garden, Zack pointing out the barns and buildings of the ranch. When they reached a corral, several young horses stood hovering over an empty watering trough. Zack casually walked over and pumped water into it.

"My, this is a big ranch," Ruthella said as she surveyed the buildings and land expanse around it.

"Yes, my father envisioned it even larger than it is now." He pointed south toward Tom's ranch. "That is Tom's and Mary Lou's ranch house up that road." He pointed to the east. "That is where Lily and Tex live. She was married to my brother, Doug, who died." He pointed west. "And that is my house, half finished and empty."

"Oh," Ruthella said and felt the hurt she heard in Zack's voice. She looked up and was swallowed in his intense eyes gazing down at her.

"I'd like to take you—and Sarah—to look at the house sometime." Zack smiled and gave a big sweep of his arm. "That and a few thousand acres all around and beyond what you can see is the Circle Z ranch."

"How wonderful! Your family should be very proud of it."

Zack smiled. "We are. My father had a great vision of what this country could be and spent a lot of time instilling it into his sons."

"He sounds like a very wise man, and you must miss him very much."

"Yes, I do." Zack nodded slowly and looked off into the distance. He turned suddenly and looked at her. "And where is your family, Ruthella?"

"I lost my mother, father, and my little brother in a

train wreck while I was away at normal school getting my teacher's certificate." She looked up into Zack's blue, blue eyes. "Other than an aunt and uncle back east, I have no other family I know of." Ruthella blushed. *Why am I telling him all this?* Her heart hammered an immediate answer. *Here is a tender man, Ruthella, a gentleman from a loving family who appreciates him. Don't be too proud, he may be the very man God has for you.* She looked up into Zack's eyes, smiled and turned to walk back to the ranch house.

"How's my son doing in school?"

Ruthella laughed. "Oh, he's delightful. I hope you know you have a very intelligent son. My biggest problem with him is keeping enough in front of him to keep his mind occupied. I am amazed at how quickly he has learned his numbers and letters."

Zack raised his eyebrows and nodded. "Glad to hear that. Maybe he'll be a lawyer some day."

They turned and walked back toward the ranch house.

"Ruthella," Zack said.

The intensity of his voice made Ruthella turn and look at him.

Suddenly Zack stopped, turned toward her and reached for her hand.

She halted beside him with questioning brows and looked up into his face. His penetrating eyes locked into her soul.

"Is it too soon to have your permission to court you?" His voice was soft and pleading. "I would like to get to know you better—and I'd like you to get to know me."

She opened her mouth but nothing came out. "I—ah—I—"

"I assure you, Ruthella, my intentions are honorable."

Ruthella stood gazing up at him, her heart turning

sommersaults, and undeniable joy bubbled within her. "Why—yes, Zack, I would like to know you better."

A big smile spread across Zack's face. He felt like a schoolboy who had just asked for his first date. "Thank you. Perhaps we could go out to dinner this coming Friday. I'll be bringing the children to school so I will talk to you later."

"Zack, Ruthella, dinner is ready." Allena hoped she had left them together long enough for something to cement.

twenty-two

Tom, Mary Lou, and the twins watched the passenger cars of the train roll by and come to a clanking stop. The conductor swung off the bottom step with his stepstool and put it in place.

They watched passenger after passenger step down then finally saw Aunt Nelda reach for the hand of the conductor and step to the ground. She turned and watched as Buck made his careful descent with the conductor's help.

Mary Lou ran to her father and threw herself into his arms. "Oh, Pa. I'm so glad to see you." The feel of his strong, familiar arms around her brought tears to her eyes.

Buck released his daughter, held her back, looked at her, and nodded. "You look well, child. It's good to see you."

Mary Lou turned, threw her arms around her aunt and squeezed her hard. "Oh, how many times I have lived this moment in my mind." She sniffed and brushed her tears away and looked from one to the other. "I can't believe you're finally here." She turned to Tom, who stood with a twin on either side of him.

Tom stepped forward and shook Buck's hand. "Glad to see you again, sir. Welcome to Texas." He hugged Aunt Nelda. "Glad you could come."

Buck stood looking at his grandson then put out his hand.

"Hello, young fella, I'm your grandfather."

Tommy hesitated for a moment and looked up at his father.

Tom nodded and gave him a nudge. "It's true. Shake hands with him, son, he's your grandfather."

Tommy placed his small hand in his grandfather's huge one, grinned sheepishly, and pumped his hand. "Hello, Grandpa."

Buck turned to Beth. "And this must be little Beth. You're a very pretty young lady and look a lot like your mama when she was a little girl." He leaned over and kissed her cheek.

Beth shied back into her mother's skirts then suddenly stepped forward and threw her arms around his neck. "Hello, Grandpa."

Grandpa. Mary Lou kept fighting a rising tide of tears that threatened to spill. An indescribable feeling of love, mixed with the joy of having her whole family together, filled her soul.

Tom helped Buck and Tommy into the front seat of the buggy and Nelda into the backseat beside Mary Lou and Beth. Each was given a piece of luggage to hold, and they were soon moving through the Texas terrain that brought back memories and favorable comments from Buck.

"I was in Texas for a while when I was a young cowboy and punched cows. Almost stayed here, but my trail boss talked me out of it."

Mary Lou feasted her eyes on her father. His hair was speckling gray, and he was more like she remembered him as a little girl, before the accident. He and Tom were talking as any two men. Aunt Nelda had said in a letter he had changed. She smiled her wonder to Aunt Nelda, who had been watching her reaction to her father.

Nelda nodded her head slowly.

Mary Lou fought tears. She was seeing her father for the first time since she was an adult. Had Aunt Nelda's tender, loving care created a miracle, or had she been too young to understand?

Nelda leaned over and whispered, "Your Pa has been going to church with me."

Mary Lou couldn't believe her ears. She looked askance at Aunt Nelda, and a couple tears finally refused to be contained and escaped down her cheeks.

The buggy finally rumbled into the main ranch yard. Allena had promised to have dinner all ready for the travelers. She also thought it would be a nice way for everyone to meet Buck and Nelda.

The minute the buggy turned into the lane the family poured out of the house and warmly welcomed the travelers. Mary Lou took baby Nellena from Allena's arms and proudly held her up for Buck and Nelda to admire. "Here, Grandpa, is your newest grandchild, we named her Nellena."

Buck reached out a finger to touch the soft rosy cheek of the baby. "She is truly a little Mary Lou," Buck observed with pride.

Allena called, "Everybody get washed up. Hattie has dinner all ready."

One by one everyone came to the table with clean hands and took their places. Mary Lou sat between Tom and her Pa. Her heart was so filled with happiness she could hardly contain it.

When they were all seated, Allena nodded to Tom.

"Let's bow our heads for prayer," he said. "Our heavenly Father, we gather round this table today with special thanks for our family gathered together. Thank you for a safe trip for Buck and Nelda and for the bounty of our land that is set before us. Help us to remember that all good things come to us through Your loving hand. We are mighty grateful this day, Lord, for all these blessings.

"Now, our Father, we ask you to bless this food to the use of our bodies and us to Thy service. In the name of our Lord and Savior, Jesus Christ. Amen."

Each head raised a smiling face.

Tom lifted a bowl of mashed potatoes, handed it to Nelda, and everybody started talking at once.

After dinner and a short visit, Tom helped Buck, Aunt Nelda, and his family into the buggy to finish their journey to their ranch house.

Mary Lou had borrowed a couple beds from Allena and Lily and set one up in Tommy's room for Pa and one in Beth's room for Aunt Nelda. As she was settling Aunt Nelda, Mary Lou asked, "Have you and Pa ever considered moving here to Texas?"

Aunt Nelda's mouth dropped open. "Move to Texas?"

"Yes, why not? There is nothing but bare subsistence for you on Pa's land. He could sell it and move here, and you could both be here with your family and let me take care of you for a change. Pa's grandchildren are here. I'd think he would want—to—be—" Mary Lou's tears refused to be contained any longer and spilled down her cheeks.

Aunt Nelda tenderly folded her arms around her niece until her sobs subsided. "I must be honest with you, child, your father is going to lose his land to back taxes. Your plans and the money to pay for this visit are godsends."

Mary Lou stared at Aunt Nelda in surprise.

"We talked to Tibby, and she said we could move in with them. It was kind of her, but I knew here's where we should be so Buck can be with his own daughter and watch his grandchildren grow up. Your father is a changed man, Mary Lou, from the last time you saw him."

Mary Lou nodded and smiled. "I can see that, Aunt Nelda."

Nelda bowed her head then looked up and smiled. Her eyes were glistening. "I've been in much prayer about this trip. But the good Lord's timing is always right." Nelda suddenly threw her hands up and covered her face. "Oh, don't let your pa know I told you all this. He'd have a fit."

Mary Lou brushed her tears away with her hands. "Why shouldn't I know? I'm his only child." She nodded. "But I know. He's a proud man, and there's nothing wrong with that. But Mama always said 'pride goeth before a fall.' Thank you, Aunt Nelda. I'm glad you told me. And I thank you for taking care of Pa for me all these years since Mama died. You and I both know that I would not be Tom's wife if it hadn't been for you and Aunt Tibby, who fought to make it possible for me to even marry Tom. Pa was agin' it. We have always been grateful for that."

The two women stared at each other, digesting what had been said.

"Let me talk to Tom and see what he says."

"Oh, I'd be delighted to move here." Nelda's face broke out into a relieved grin that eased some of the new worry lines Mary Lou saw in her face. She heaved a big sigh. "I can't tell you how glad I am we are here. I feel that what Buck needs now is the touch of his daughter and family in his life. He's fought through his anger of the accident that crippled him. What he needs now is to be a grandfather and see his grandchildren grow up. He needs that hope."

"And I need my family here. I *want* my family here." Mary Lou admitted. "I know Tom feels the same way I do. He has always had a kind, defensive word for Pa."

By the time the women and Tom had the beds ready, everyone was ready to fall into them.

As Mary Lou slid into bed beside Tom, she cuddled up to his back.

He turned and took her into his arms and kissed her.

"We have some talking to do," Mary Lou said softly.

"I know, but it can wait until tomorrow. It has been a big day."

Mary Lou sighed and snuggled. "A wonderful day."

The next time Tom kissed her, she was asleep.

twenty-three

Zack turned the buggy onto the road to his house. He glanced over at Ruthella, who sat prim and proper beside him. When he had gone to get Ruthella and Sarah this morning, Sarah hadn't been feeling good and had taken to her bed.

Ruthella had said she couldn't go either.

It had taken some convincing talk, with Sarah's help, to get Ruthella to agree that it would be all right for her and Zack to visit his house without Sarah. They wouldn't be there alone. The carpenters would be there.

Zack pulled the buggy to a halt, flipped the reins around the whip, hopped out, and helped Ruthella to the ground. "The outside is completely finished, and the inside is coming right along and is ready for paint and wallpaper."

The carpenters were busy at their work.

Zack glanced at Ruthella. "I'm now at the point where I need a woman's opinion about things."

Ruthella smiled and admired the resemblance of the house to some of the eastern homes she was familiar with. "It looks beautiful from the outside, and I'm impressed with the inside," she said. Her heart did another one of the odd, little flutterings she had been putting up with all morning.

Zack tucked his arm through hers and helped her over the uneven ground and up the wide porch steps. She recognized the touch of the southern plantation look. She could picture white wicker chairs with flowered cushions in them spread across the porch.

As they stepped into the entry hall Zack led her to the banister of a large, wide, sweeping staircase that led to the second floor. The rail curved up and around, exposing the upstairs walls with four bedroom doors. Zack guided her through the rooms and made comments on how pleased he was that the men had done so well and had finished much more than he realized.

As they walked through the upstairs bedrooms, Ruthella pictured each one in her mind with four-poster beds covered with quilted comforters and long floral draperies at the windows. When they came back downstairs her mind placed the hall benches and the coat hanging racks. The parlour was big enough to take a large-size sofa and she imagined lace curtains and brocade draperies at the tall windows. The kitchen wasn't too big—just big enough—with a hugh fireplace on one wall. She would put. . . What was she doing? She blushed and realized she was furnishing the house in her mind!

"The kitchen will have a well right outside the back door. Many of the new homes in the east are starting to have water brought right into the home by pipes. I'm looking into that."

"Why, that would be wonderful!" Ruthella answered and felt her cheeks flush warm again.

They circled back to the entryway and walked out on the porch.

Zack stopped, turned to Ruthella, and grinned. "Well, what do you think of it?"

"Oh, Zack, it is elegant! Any woman would be thrilled having—a—home like—this." She felt her face grow warm with a blush.

"I'm glad you like it. But I'm not interested in *any*

woman." He picked up her hands and pulled her to face him. "Ruthella—"

Ruthella's heart fluttered. She stared at the buttons on his coat and held her breath.

Zack lifted her chin and gazed down into her eyes. "Ruthella, I'm tired of playing games and trying to be so diplomatic. I have to know. Do you care for me at all?"

The words exploded into the air and sounded like beautiful music to Ruthella's ears. She slowly, bravely released her hold on her feelings and looked up into Zack's eyes and let her love pour through hers. "Yes, Zack, I admire you very much."

Zack shook his head. "I don't mean *admire*, Ruthella. I'm in love with you and wonder if you could ever return that love."

Ruthella had been waiting for a long time to hear those words, the most beautiful words she had ever heard in all her life and until now had begun to wonder if she would ever hear them said to her. She allowed her heart to speak. "Yes, Zack, I've loved you for quite some time, but this is the first time I've had the courage to admit it, even to myself."

Zack swept her into his arms and pressed his lips against hers. He kissed her again and again then held her back and smiled at her, his eyes flashing.

Ruthella lowered her eyelids. She could feel the blush on her face but it didn't matter. She tilted her face again to receive his kiss and clung to him.

They parted, turned, and looked at the room around them. All of a sudden it began to look like home.

Zack put his around around her waist, and they turned and began a new walk through what would be their home.

Suddenly, Ruthella stopped. "Oh, Sarah. . ."

"What about Sarah?"

"Oh, Zack, what will she do? She can't live in that little cabin all alone."

"Well, than she'll just have to come and live in one of these rooms. It's a pretty big house. I think we could find one."

Ruthella's eyes glistened as she looked up into his face. "Oh, Zack, thank you. I couldn't have left her alone. I had planned to just have her as my helper even though they could no longer pay her for teaching. If she wasn't teaching, what could she do? She has taught me so much. A country school where you have full charge is a lot different from being a teacher in one of the schools of the east, where you are responsible for only one room." Ruthella laughed. "I've learned what sticks and logs to hunt for to build a good fire, when it's time for the berries to ripen and where they are, to take the children berry picking so they can eat fresh fruit for lunch, I've. . ." Ruthella laughed then suddenly quieted and stared seriously into Zack's eyes. "You will let me keep on teaching. . .won't you?"

"It means that much to you?"

"Oh, yes. Zack, I promise you, I can be a wife and a schoolteacher, too."

Zack pulled her into his arms. "If you want to teach school, then you teach and I'll help you all I can."

Ruthella threw her arms around his neck and hugged him hard. "Thank you. Thank you."

"And—after we're married—after our honeymoon—" Zack grinned, "we'll move Sarah right in with us. I agree she'd never be able to fend for herself in that little cabin. Besides she can keep you company when I have to be away at the legislature for weeks or a month at a time."

The heavy weight on Ruthella's chest changed to a feather and floated away. She threw her arms around Zack's neck and hugged him hard. "Oh, Zack, thank you."

On the way home, they talked and made plans. Zack pulled into the Circle Z and looked at Ruthella. "I want to stop and share our good news with Mother, and we both need to talk to Zachary."

Ruthella agreed.

As they walked into the kitchen, Hattie lifted a pie from the oven.

"No wonder it smells so good in here," Zack said.

"Give it a half an hour and you can have a piece," Hattie said as she set it on a cooling rack.

"I'll wait! Where's Mother?"

"Here I am." Allena beamed as she stepped from the hallway.

"Ruthella, how nice to see you." She looked behind her. "Where's Sarah?"

Ruthella blushed. "She wasn't feeling good this morning."

"Oh, then, you didn't see Zack's house." Allena's face fell.

Zack smiled. "Yes, we did, Mother, and we have something to tell you. Ruthella not only loves the house, she loves me and has accepted my offer of marriage."

Allena face first showed shock, then pleasant surprise. "Oh, that is the best news I've had in a long time." She threw her arms around Ruthella. "My dear, I'm not only happy for you but for me, too."

Hattie was all smiles. "Well now, ain't that grand." She patted Zack on the back and said, "It's about time. I was afraid you was going to let this good girl get away!"

Everyone laughed. Leave it to Hattie. Nothing ever got past her, yet whenever you asked her a question, she never knew a thing. At one time or another everyone in the family had learned that she was the only one in the family who could keep a secret.

Allena suddenly frowned. "Oh, but—but what about Sarah?"

"No buts," Zack said. "She'll come and live with us, and she and Ruthella will continue teaching just as they are now."

Allena gazed at her oldest son. He grew more like his father every day.

twenty-four

Mary Lou grabbed her empty water buckets and went out to the well, filled them, and set them by the door. She was tired so decided to seize the rare opportunity to sit down on her restin' chair. It felt good just to sit. She had scrubbed and hung clothes all morning, her baby was finally napping, the twins were in school, Pa had ridden out on one of the hay wagons with Tom, and Aunt Nelda was down visiting Allena. She relished these few rare moments alone.

Movement caught her attention. Lily was halfway between the main ranch and heading in her direction. Mary Lou waved, and Lily answered with a wave of what looked like a letter in her hand. "Thought you'd like to see this," Lily said as she neared and handed Mary Lou the letter. She backed up and dropped to the ground, crisscrossed her legs, and covered them with her skirt.

"It's from Isobel!" Mary Lou cried, opened it and spread out the sheet of school paper it was written on.

Lily nodded. "Read it aloud. I'm anxious to hear how she is."

> *"Dear Mary Lou and Lily,*
> *"My mother was very glad you gave me your address so we could write and thank you for your kind care of me. My mother and father say they will never be able to thank you two ladies enough for your kindness and concern for someone you didn't*

even know.

"I am working at Mrs. Landeau's millinery shop, and she says I have a God-given natural talent for sewing. I have made several hats that have sold right away. I want to say thank-you and God bless you both for saving me from that horrible life of sin. I took your advice, Lily, 'the least said is the easiest mended.' I haven't told the details.

"I have a nice young man I went to school with who has been taking me to picnics and we go to church together. He has hinted he likes me but hasn't said so. He has always been a shy boy.

"Say hello to everybody for me. God bless and keep you all.

"Your grateful Christian friend,
"Isobel"

Mary Lou looked up through a veil of mist.

Lily's tears had wet her cheeks.

Mary Lou handed the letter to Lily. "Why don't you keep this letter, Lily? You were really the one who helped her. I just happened to find her in my barn and didn't have the faintest idea of what to do. So God sent you."

Lily smiled, took the letter, tucked it in her pocket, and got up. She didn't try to hide her tears. She walked over and put her arms around Mary Lou, hugged her, and left for home.

Mary Lou watched Lily walk slowly back to the main ranch house to get her daughter, Genevieve, and thanked God for that sinner turned saint God had given her for a sister.

A faint baby's cry brought Mary Lou to her feet, and she went in to check on her baby daughter. She lifted little Paula into her arms. She was such a tiny thing. Allena had named her. Paula means, little or small and it had also been her grandmother's name. Mary Lou and Tom had liked it, it seemed to suit her, so Paula Nellena she became.

She sat down in the rocker and nursed Paula and thought of all the changes that had come about in the past year. Their family was growing all the time. Mary Lou lifted her heart in praise to God for her pa and aunt Nelda being here. She felt more settled, like a mother hen when all her chicks are safe in the nest. They both seemed happy, and she couldn't get over the change in Pa. He even sang the hymns in church. For the first time in all her life she could now see why Mama fell in love with him, and it made her heart happy to see Tom and Pa talking and working together. She gently laid little Paula in the cradle so as not to wake her.

She heard men talking and before long Tom and Pa came in.

"Shhhhhh!" She put her finger across her lips to quiet their talking, and their voices dropped to just above a whisper. Mary Lou hurried and dished up three steaming plates of stew and dumplings from the simmering pot on the stove and placed them in front of the men and herself and sat down.

After Tom said grace he turned to her. "What have you been doing today?" Tom asked her.

"We got a letter from Isobel, and she is fine."

"Glad to hear that," Tom nodded and grinned. "Well your pa and I checked out the old cabin, and he says he likes the idea of he and Nelda living there; then it won't make it too crowded here."

"Yep. It's good and sound. It will do fine," Pa said. He grinned. "And that way Nelda can have some of her things out around her. She says it makes her feel more homelike."

"But Pa, it'll need some fixin'," Mary Lou said.

"We and the boys can do that," Tom said.

"Well, you fix it and Aunt Nelda and I will clean it."

"Good 'nuf," Tom said.

The men finished and went back out to fix one of the wagons.

It did her heart good to see Tom working with her pa. As Mary Lou watched she noticed Pa walked different. He still had his limp that swung his body from side to side, but his head was up, his shoulders straighter. Yep, as Aunt Nelda said, since Pa became a Christian he had become a new and different man—more so than she had ever seen him. Mary Lou's heart sang for the joy of having her family here, with her. She looked up. *Oh, Mama, Pa is here, and our children are going to have a grandpa. I wish you were here, too.* The tears she shed were for joy unspeakable.

A Letter To Our Readers

Dear Reader:

In order that we might better contribute to your reading enjoyment, we would appreciate your taking a few minutes to respond to the following questions. When completed, please return to the following:

Rebecca Germany, Managing Editor
Heartsong Presents
P.O. Box 719
Uhrichsville, Ohio 44683

1. Did you enjoy reading *A Heart for Home?*
   ❑ Very much. I would like to see more books
      by this author!
   ❑ Moderately
      I would have enjoyed it more if _____

   _____

2. Are you a member of **Heartsong Presents**? ❑Yes ❑No
   If no, where did you purchase this book?_____

   _____

3. What influenced your decision to purchase this
   book? (Check those that apply.)

   ❑ Cover   ❑ Back cover copy

   ❑ Title   ❑ Friends

   ❑ Publicity   ❑ Other_____

4. How would you rate, on a scale from 1 (poor) to 5
   (superior), the cover design?_____

5. On a scale from 1 (poor) to 10 (superior), please rate the following elements.

    ___Heroine   ___Plot

    ___Hero   ___Inspirational theme

    ___Setting   ___Secondary characters

6. What settings would you like to see covered in **Heartsong Presents** books?_____

_____

_____

7. What are some inspirational themes you would like to see treated in future books?_____

_____

_____

8. Would you be interested in reading other **Heartsong Presents** titles? ❏ Yes   ❏ No

9. Please check your age range:
  ❏ Under 18   ❏ 18-24   ❏ 25-34
  ❏ 35-45   ❏ 46-55   ❏ Over 55

10. How many hours per week do you read? _____

Name _____

Occupation _____

Address _____

City_____ State_____ Zip _____

·····Heart♥ng·····

HEARTSONG PRESENTS TITLES AVAILABLE NOW:

(If ordering from this page, please remember to include it with the order form.)

·········Presents·········

Heart♥ng Presents
Love Stories Are Rated G!

That's for godly, gratifying, and of course, great! If you love a thrilling love story, but don't appreciate the sordidness of some popular paperback romances, **Heartsong Presents** is for you. In fact, **Heartsong Presents** is the *only inspirational romance book club*, the only one featuring love stories where Christian faith is the primary ingredient in a marriage relationship.

Sign up today to receive your first set of four, never before published Christian romances. Send no money now; you will receive a bill with the first shipment. You may cancel at any time without obligation, and if you aren't completely satisfied with any selection, you may return the books for an immediate refund!

Imagine. . .four new romances every four weeks—two historical, two contemporary—with men and women like you who long to meet the one God has chosen as the love of their lives. . .all for the low price of $9.97 postpaid.

To join, simply complete the coupon below and mail to the address provided. **Heartsong Presents** romances are rated G for another reason: They'll arrive *Godspeed!*